In Encounters

Book 1: The Hero of my Love Scene

Nicki Grace

Copyright © 2020 KGA Sound

All rights reserved.

ISBN: 9798685965721

Inevitable Encounters: The Hero of my Love Scene

DEDICATION

To my sister and best friend Deni. I love you more than you will ever know and I thank you for always being one of my biggest cheerleaders. Life wouldn't be the same without you and if there is anyone in the world who deserves a happily ever after, it's you.

Chapter 1
Winter

Winter gawked at how big his dick was because… it was huge. Instinctively, she wondered if he knew how to use it but quickly decided no. Nothing against the guy, but in her sexual experience, big dicks didn't equal big orgasms. If she was completely honest, regardless of the size of a man's package or the position they delivered it in, it never got her anywhere. Therefore, the dick before her may as well have been nothing more than a prop like those used at her job, "Movie Box Studios" appearing useful on set but useless in reality.

However, capabilities aside, she had to admit it was impressive. Bouncing around and swinging back and forth like it was parting the way for a famous celebrity to come through. Who knows, maybe the guy it was attached to was famous, or at least pretended to be as a day job because he had the look. Tall and muscular with a chocolate complexion and a flirtatious smile, his aura screamed, "star" or "groupies apply here." Still, she doubted he was famous, although his dick could be, the guy it was attached to was a male dancer hired by her friend, Jessica, as a celebratory token for Chloe's bachelorette party.

She giggled as the dancing dick brought to mind a handheld compass with the arrow, pointing and shifting uncontrollably in all different directions. There was a second dick present. It belonged to the other male dancer of the night. Although it wasn't as big, it too was impressive.

But instead of being fun and extra bouncy like the compass dick, this one was more well behaved and of the no-nonsense variety. It pointed straight out and barely bounced. It was as if it refused to have a good time and had been brought to the party against its will. Every move the dancer made that attempted to send it in any position besides forward-facing was met with challenge—talk about stubborn.

If it wasn't clear before, it was clear now. She was most definitely tipsy… possibly, even drunk. With that being said, at least she was in good company because inebriated was the current status for most of the women in the room.

About 20 feet ahead was Chloe, the bride-to-be, and one of Winter's best friends. Chloe had her wild meter on full blast. She was dancing and waving dollars in the air yelling, "Sexy Chocolate! Sexy Chocolate!" at the top of her lungs with two other girls.

Having their wish granted, one of the chocolate eye candies took a break from the group of girls he was entertaining and started heading their way. He was most certainly making sure to keep all eyes on him as he strutted, twisted and danced his firm ass all the way over to Chloe and her back up screamers.

As Winter sat there lounging, drink in hand and enjoying a much-needed break from all the excitement, she was thankful they were in the penthouse suite of a five-star hotel. The noise level coming from this room alone would have earned them non-stop complaints. Around fifteen of Chloe's closest female family and friends were scattered around the beautiful lavish suite that housed a living room, dining room, kitchen and three bedrooms.

The party was being held in the living room area. It was a grand layout that offered more than enough space to accommodate their needs. Impeccable decor in golds, silvers and whites offered an expensive, bold look to the room. Floor-to-ceiling windows and an oversized balcony provided incredible views of the city. Thankfully the windows included curtains because no matter how high up they were, this party needed no chance of falling into the category of public viewing.

Modern but classic couches that were a staple in the suite's daily decor hugged the room walls. They had been pushed aside to make room for three round tables that could seat up to six women each. In addition to the round tables, there were three gold mini tables placed in close proximity. One displayed the cake, the second held bridal presents and the third was home to various gag gifts such as tiny bottles of alcohol and keychain dildos.

Once the space requirements were met, the hotel spared no expense in providing proper servers for the event. The staff was responsible for serving, cooking and cleaning before, after and during the party. Winter could tell the staff was operating at the top of their game tonight.

They made sure everything remained immaculate. If an empty glass, loose napkins, or random trash was dropped or left behind, it was almost instantly properly discarded. In addition, and without request, the staff kept drink refills continuous. Although a short list of finger foods, the menu was fresh, delicious and of the highest quality.

The music was blasting, "I'm in Love with a Stripper" by T-Pain, and the good vibes were present. Things had already been in full swing for over two hours and it seemed that the party could continue on for just as long.

Taking the final sip of her third apple martini of the night, Winter realized how good she felt. Her whole body was warm and completely relaxed. As she savored the sweet, yet slightly sour taste on her tongue, she couldn't remember the last time before tonight that she'd had a drink. She would need to remember to make this a regular thing. A yummy alcoholic drink would be a welcomed delight as a way to unwind after a long work week.

Continuing to scan the room and observe the male dancers earn their tips, she spotted Jessica. She was re-stacking gifts that had fallen over or shifted out of place. Jessica was an event planner and the one responsible for this fabulously X-rated event. Based on her all over the place movements, she was still very much on event planner duty. One would think that she would take a moment to enjoy the party, but Jessica was a host through and through.

She was all about details and keeping things in order. Some would call her uptight, but that wasn't entirely true. She was actually fun, kind and simply loved her job. Probably more so than Winter loved hers, and that was saying something. Jessica was known to enjoy the planning more than the event itself, and even though this event was the bridal shower of one of her dearest friends, it was no exception. Looking up to see Winter watching her, Jessica gave a quick thumbs up and moved on to another task.

A few feet behind Jessica was the bar area. Winter noticed one of the servers holding a tray and leaning against the bar staring at her. Another staff member behind the counter was making more drinks, so it was a safe assumption that the guy undressing her with his eyes was waiting for them to be ready so that he could bring them over. Their eyes locked, and he winked at her; in return, she offered a kind smile.

He probably thought her smile meant more than it did, but he would be mistaken. She had dated some very handsome men, and although the stories started out different, they always ended the same.

"Not tonight, buddy," she thought.

Tonight was reserved for fun and friends. Her only interest was making sure that Chloe had the best night of her life. She wasn't looking for any men to flirt with or even date at the moment. Last she checked, her love life had flatlined and she had no plans to try and resuscitate it. Instead, she was taking a break, a sort of hiatus from relationships, and that break included sex.

She wasn't bitter about it or even saddened. It was simple, really. As of about a year ago, she'd had the realization that her focus was way too locked in on trying to find "the right guy." Not wanting to be the type of woman that was always looking for a man, she decided to try something new. That new thing was to try nothing at all. Just enjoy life and all the great things it had to offer. She was tired, anyway. One way or another, true love would find her; it was all about timing. If it didn't… well, that was a worry for another day.

The reference to timing as it pertained to love made her think of her mom, who passed away from cancer a couple of years ago. It was a horrible loss for Winter as she experienced it much too soon behind the loss of her dad to a stroke the year before that. She missed them deeply and often thought of them.

Their love was of proportions greater than she had ever seen. The way they took care of each other and enjoyed one another's company was something more commonly seen between best friends instead of husband and wife. By watching them, she learned how powerful and fulfilling true love can be. It was something so magnetic, words couldn't describe it. If she could find love that came anywhere close to what her parents had, she'd consider herself to be the luckiest girl in the world. To accept anything less would not only be a disservice to herself, but disrespectful to her parents' memory and all they had taught her.

Winter was really close to her mom. They spent a lot of time together going antique shopping, watching movies and having great conversations. Their favorite movies were, "The Breakfast Club" and "Girls Trip".

Whenever Winter would get sad or feel down, she would visit her mom, and they'd pop in a movie and eat loads of junk food until Winter felt better. Her mom just always seemed to know what to do and what to say to get Winter through tough times.

When she asked her mom why she chose Winter as her name, her mom said it was her favorite season. However, Winter knew that her mom was biased to the season because it was during a cold, snowy day in February that her mom's car broke down, and Winter's dad, a stranger to her mom at the time, pulled over to help her. They'd been inseparable ever since.

When she would vent about struggles in the love department, her mom would make her feel better by reminding her that, just like her name, everything had its season, and her season for love would come.

Well, it hadn't come, not for love anyway. It seemed every relationship she entered ended in disaster. When she was younger, she thought that by now, being 31, all areas in her life would be in order.

It's not that she was one of those people that presumed entering into her thirties would magically make everything ok. It's was just that from early on, she had planned and made choices that she assumed would have gotten her everything on her checklist of life. She'd always been a great deal more serious than most of her friends once they graduated from high school.

Instead of partying and procrastinating, she picked up second and third jobs so that she could pay off college debts and buy her first house as soon as possible.

She wanted a job in the film industry and landed her dream position about seven years ago when she started working as a prop master for Movie Box Studios.

To date, she had paid off the college debts, landed the dream job and gotten the house. But the guy… he seemed to be missing in action. Assuming he was having trouble finding her or maybe she wasn't open-minded enough, she decided to cast a wide net with her dating choices.

God forbid he fall through the cracks because he was unemployed, underemployed, wasn't tall enough, romantic enough or seemed a bit weird in the beginning. She even had a couple of long-distance relationships because love knew no bounds, and if she never tried, she would never know.

Basically, she let the fear of losing her dream guy before getting to know him drive her, and she had paid for it dearly.

Her dating choices over the years were poor and, sometimes, downright comical. Her attempts to roll with the punches and move on to the next guy who might give her the love story she so desperately wanted was a big mistake.

Instead, she kept reliving the same dating horror stories that left her in the role of the hopeful leading lady and rotated the position of leading asshole to different men. To be fair, it wasn't always the guy's fault; she was just as guilty for choosing such poor mates, to begin with.

Once, she dated a guy named Carl, who she thought was going places. Sadly, the only place he was going was from his mom's couch to hers. As an excuse for his couch living lifestyle, he told her he was only living with his mom as a temporary arrangement until builders finished the construction on his five-bedroom house.

The problem was, he happened to leave out the small details that, due to his poor credit score, he didn't qualify for a loan and that there was no actual house being built, just a hypothetical one. When confronted about this, he called it being a visionary and said that his only fault was wanting a woman he could build with. In the end, she didn't know if he was a compulsive liar or just delusional, but she decided to let him sort it out alone.

Then there was Greg, a magician. True, it was an odd job, and the idea of it didn't exactly make Winter giddy, but he was sweet, charming and very funny. They met at a local comedy club and connected over their love for old school comedians. They dated for close to two years, and she fell in love with him.

Things were going so well that she felt certain that there were wedding bells in their future. Wanting to be the supportive girlfriend, she didn't bat an eye when he suddenly stopped being interested in having sex with her. His job was hectic, he'd said. With so many tricks to learn and places to perform, it was really messing with his drive.

She idiotically accepted his explanation in hopes that improvement was right around the corner. Besides, him no longer wanting sex didn't stop his charming words and romantic gestures, so, in her mind, he was worth fighting for. She eventually found that he was using all that romance and charm to slide out of her bed and into everyone else's. He was a serial cheater who was as equally talented at pulling rabbits out of hats as he was with pulling excuses out of his ass.

Next was Alex. Maybe, just maybe, things could have worked with Alex. He was a good guy and did well for himself. There was just one problem. His dick was too small, minuscule, really. He had some kind of condition that affected the size of it. She felt really bad for him and tried to tough it out. In an attempt to keep her happy, he was more than eager to engage in oral stimulation, but he was terrible at it! Like Guinness World Record bad. Coming to the conclusion that never having experienced an orgasm didn't mean she had to keep being a victim to his tongue of torture, she cut her losses. After it was all said and done, she, or more so, her vagina, moved on and couldn't be any happier.

Eventually, and rightfully frustrated that yet another love dream had turned into a nightmare, it was time to call it quits... at least for a while. It seemed no matter what sacrifice she made or how promising the guy seemed, it never worked out. Her heart and mind needed a rest.

When or if the right guy came along, she would deal with it then. Her biggest fear was that she would fuck it up. Being lied to and let down repeatedly had its way of making her doubt most things guys say. Her track record proved she gave men way too much benefit and not nearly enough doubt. Therefore, she wasn't sure she could trust her own dating judgment.

But love was tricky. She had to balance protecting her heart while not becoming a woman that let their past hurt dictate their future, but that was hard. Somehow fixing her broken heart time after time made her weary, and she was always waiting for the other shoe to drop because eventually it would drop and kick her in the ass.

The server depositing another apple martini in front of her broke her thought process. She looked up at him. It was the guy that'd been staring at her.

Now that he was up close, she could see his teeth were in dire need of some dental attention.

"Having a nice night?" he asked.

She smiled and said, "yes, it's lovely. I've been looking forward to this so I could get a break from my five kids. The single mom's life is a hard one," she lied.

She saw his expression change like someone had thrown cold water in his face.

Trying to cover his reaction, he said. "I'll bet, well, enjoy your night." Then, he picked up her empty glass and almost ran away.

She giggled to herself. He couldn't get out of there fast enough. She raised a glass to basically his trail of dust and then took a giant sip.

The night remained something for the memory books for another few hours. Little by little, the party downsized until no one was left but Chloe, Winter, Jessica and Chloe's Twin cousins, Talia and Tina. The girls were in Chloe's bridal shower and also staying overnight, putting the three luxury rooms to use. The bride-to-be had one room, the twins shared a room and Winter and Jessica had the third room.

Deciding it was time to turn in, Winter headed towards her bedroom for the night. Jessica was already in their room asleep because being the wedding planner meant that she had busy work tomorrow. Talia and Tina had gone to their rooms about an hour before with the intent to return but never did. It seemed that Talia went to pee, but because she'd had quite a few drinks, Tina found her asleep sitting on the toilet.

That just left Chloe and Winter. Last Winter saw Chloe was about an hour ago. Chloe was sitting in a chair on the balcony at the time, having an in-depth (and more than likely) raunchy phone conversation with her fiancé, Derek.

As she walked across the living room, she ran into Chloe. Literally almost ran into her because Chloe was running towards Winter with her arms open and collided with her. Embracing Winter on impact, Chloe was obviously still drunk and riding on her happy emotions. Winter had sobered up a little while ago because she had let her fourth drink of the night be her last.

"I thought you were on the phone outside on the balcony?" Winter asked, holding on to Chloe more so to keep her steady than anything else.

"No, silly," Chloe replied, swaying a bit. "I went to my room a little while ago, had to have a private chat with the soon to be Mister, if you know what I mean." Chloe attempted a wink that manifested in her basically closing both eyes for about 5 seconds.

"Enough said," Winter responded.

"I just love you guys so much," Chloe slurred. "This was the best night ever! Thank you for everything, Wint."

Then she leaned in close and said, "don't tell everyone else, but you know you are my favorite season?"

Winter smiled. Chloe had been saying that quirky line to her ever since they met in 4th grade. It was her cutesy way of telling Winter that she was her favorite person.

"Your secret's safe with me," she said. "You know we'd do anything for our best friend in the world, the magnificent Chloe Fosters. Oh wait, I meant Chloe James."

Chloe giggled, "It does have a nice ring to it, doesn't it?"

"It does."

Chloe let go and extended her arm upward and to the left.

"Guess I'll head back to my room now. Tomorrow, a weeding awaits."

Grabbing her friend by the shoulder and positioning her body to the right, Winter said, "no, Chloe, your room is that way. And yes, a wedding awaits tomorrow, not a weeding."

Chloe hiccuped and said, "Oops, my bad," and walked very unbalanced toward her room.

Chapter 2
Winter

The next morning, there were people everywhere, getting the girls ready for the big day. Once again, all the action took place in the living room. They were being styled and made runway beautiful by a highly ranked beauty team provided by the hotel.

As far as the prepping went, everyone was getting the same services, just in a different order. For instance, while Chloe, the overly pampered bride, was getting a pedicure and manicure, Winter, the maid of honor, was getting her hair done, and Talia and Tina, the bridesmaids, were getting their brows waxed and eyelash extensions applied.

Jessica, who couldn't hold a position in the wedding party because she was the wedding planner, ensured that everyone stayed the course and all items were delivered on schedule.

Winter was surprised that no one had a hangover after such a wild night. Chloe and her cousins must have been some pro drinkers because once the alarms went off and they had finished their in-suite breakfast, Chloe, Talia and Tina were energetic, excited and ready to tackle the day.

"Hey, Winter," Talia said, sitting utterly still as to not cause a mistake with her brow shaping. "How'd you sleep?"

"Good. Not as good as you, though. I heard you fell asleep on the toilet."

"Girl, yes! One minute I was peeing; the next, Tina was shaking me. I have no idea when it happened. I should have been more responsible like you and sat my ass down a whole lot earlier."

"I only sat down cause I was hurting from the whiplash I'd developed watching those dicks swing around."

At that comment, all the girls laughed.

"You're right," Tina chimed in. "Now that you mentioned it, I think my neck hurts too."

"Mine too," Chloe and Talia added in unison.

They all laughed again and then settled back into their scheduled steps of the bridal party beautification process. Nearly every thirty minutes, one of them switched stations until each of them had been plucked, packed, painted and primped. If it was in the name of beauty, then it was done.

The outcome was four women who looked red carpet-worthy. As they took tons of selfies and group photos, they would forever remember that for Chloe's wedding, they looked like beauty queens.

Even though Winter loved it, she wasn't interested in being primped to perfection again anytime soon. She was more laid back in her style and preferred minimal makeup. Full-fledged makeup was ok when the occasion called for it, but it wasn't her go-to for day-to-day. Even still, she did look amazing. Her lavender dress was simple and elegant, and the silver, light studded shoes were a flawless touch.

Odd though, that the shoes fit a little snug. Taking them off and checking the size, she saw the 8 printed inside the shoe label plain as day. Shrugging it off, she figured maybe they would be ok after walking in them a bit.

By the time the wedding began, the heels Winter was wearing were killing her feet. They were clearly a size too small, and she found herself wincing with every step. However, not wanting to create any issues on Chloe's special day or give Jessica a full-on aneurysm concerning one tiny detail being out of place, she decided to tough through it.

Besides, whose fault was it that this size 8 fit her like a size 7 in the types of shoes she was used to wearing?

It's not like Jessica hadn't dropped off her dress and shoes and told her to try them on weeks before the wedding to make sure everything fit correctly. She tried on the dress and got sidetracked with something and totally forgot about the shoes. When Jessica checked back with her, she told her everything was fine. She did see the shoes were a size 8, so she assumed there shouldn't be an issue.

She was very wrong in her assumption. Taking the walk down the aisle to stand in her designated position, she forced herself to smile through the stinging in her eyes as a tear threatened to roll down her face due to the extreme discomfort.

Not giving in to the pain, Winter gracefully made it to her position, managing to quash the impulse to yank off her shoes and throw them into the crowd. She stood tall and proud, and just by looking at her, no one would ever know she was wearing size 8 torture devices. To keep her mind off the matter, she mentally cursed the shoe company repeatedly.

However, when Chloe entered the room, Winter momentarily forgot about the pain.

Her friend looked gorgeous and very chic—like a flawless, golden brown doll created for the sole purpose of being admired. Not a hair was out of place. Chloe's high cheekbones, full lips and exotic light brown eyes were the picture of perfection. Her classic look paired well with the timeless elegance that the entire theme displayed.

Winter couldn't help but hope that she too would know what it felt like to be a bride one day. Until then, she knew no one more deserving of love than Chloe. Her heart swelled with happiness for her friend.

As Derek and Chloe read their wedding vows and made promises to love, cherish and honor one another, Winter was grateful to have such touching words to cover her tears because the pain of her feet was back at the forefront of her mind.

When the wedding was over and the reception was in full swing, all bets were off. Winter tossed the shoes aside and danced the night away. Mimicking Winter's display, Talia and Tina joined in, tossing their shoes to the side as well and jumping on the dance floor.

Even Jessica joined in on the dancing and abandoned her planner responsibilities when her favorite Lil Wayne song, "A Milli," came on. Jessica and Chloe cleared the dance floor as they shook their asses and performed a fun dance routine they had come up with for the song. The whole time the crowd watched and cheered them on.

All and all, it was a really fun night, and just like the night before, Winter ended up tipsy. She blamed the twins for her current state through laughs and slurs for urging her to try a drink that they swore to Winter "didn't contain much alcohol."

Whether they were honest or deceptive in their attempts to include Winter in the good time they were having, she didn't know. However, after consuming two drinks, she was no longer sober. Luckily, she was taking an Uber home, so she didn't have to worry about driving.

As the night came to an end and all the goodbyes were said, Chloe left for her honeymoon with Derek. Winter exited the building shortly after Chloe, hugging her friends goodbye and promising to text when she made it in.

When the Uber driver, Keith, she thinks that's what he said his name was, pulled up in front of her house, he looked back at her.

"Ma'am, do you need any help?"

"No, no," she said, waving his question aside. "I'm fine."

She pushed the door, which felt like it weighed a ton, open and stuck one wobbly leg out onto the ground. She was no longer highly tipsy, but sober also wasn't an adequate description. When she was completely out of the car, she was surprised at how well she was standing. Putting one foot in front of the other, she began what seemed like a long journey to her front door.

Continuing her left foot, right foot rhythm, Winter mentally cheered herself on. If she could keep her focus, she might make it to the door without falling flat on her face.

In what seemed like a far off distance behind her, she heard the Uber drive pull off.

Almost instantly, she regretted shifting her concentration even that slight bit. She put another foot forward and stepped onto the raised concrete that had been an eyesore on her walking path for years. Too late to catch her balance, she stumbled forward and fell. She was grateful that on instinct, she had put her hands out. It provided a cushion to the fall, and all the weight was placed on her right hand.

Carefully, she got up and made it the rest of the way to the door. She was so tired, and all she wanted was to crawl into bed and sleep forever. Inside, she went to the bathroom and checked out her hand.

Besides the fact that it was really tender, it didn't look too bad. A few light scratches here and there that bled but would likely not leave a scar. Too tired to do much else, Winter typed out a quick "home now" text to her friends, pulled her clothes and shoes off, wrapped a hand towel around her injured hand and fell into the bed.

◆◆◆

She woke up the next morning to banging.

"Ugh," she thought. "What was that, and what will make it stop?"

Turning over slowly and opening her eyes slightly to avoid letting in too much light, she looked at the clock. The display read 8:45am.

She had a terrible headache. What was in that drink? She was going to kill those damn twins the next time she saw them. She loved them like family, but she was still going to kill them.

Mentally, she thanked Chloe for having a wedding and reception on a Saturday. She most certainly couldn't go to work feeling like this. Having Sunday as a buffer to wind down from a wild night was exactly what she needed.

That and an ibuprofen, because in addition to the hammering that was happening in her head, her right hand felt tender and stiff. She looked down at it, and the memory of her falling came back to her. Goodness, she felt awful.

"BANG BANG BANG!!!"

Then there was that. The loud irritating noise. She sat up and almost toppled out of bed. Dragging herself to the window that faced the neighboring house, she peeked out of the blinds and immediately saw the culprit.

Workers were doing construction on the house that had been on the market for a few months now. Two guys were on the roof, and several others were unloading boxes and windows off of trucks.

If she wasn't feeling so yucky, she might have taken a bit longer to enjoy the view. Almost all of them were wearing tanks and sporting arms that would make a girl want to ask for hugs in lieu of hellos.

"BANG!!! BANG!!!"

The guys on the roof were at it again. Making all that noise when a girl just needed some sleep.

"Talia and Tina were already in for it. Adding the two roof guys to the list shouldn't be such a big deal," she thought, annoyed.

Winter sighed. May as well get the day started. Possibly when she'd made herself a quick bite to eat and taken a pain pill, she would feel better. As for now, a cup of coffee was the only thing that would keep her from murdering those damn men on the roof.

Chapter 3
Kody

Kody was in a good mood—an exceptionally good mood. This was to be expected when he began a new home renovation project, and with this house being almost a complete gut job, his exceptional mood would likely last all week.

Nothing against new construction homes because his company Haven Construction did handle contracts for both, but renovations were just somehow different. Truth be told, they were the reason he started the company in the first place. Something about seeing a home go from "waste" to "worth" really made him feel accomplished, which was a good thing because this current project would require his third move in 6 months.

Moving around that often was very inconvenient, but it was also rare, so he didn't mind. Usually, work within his company kept him in one state at least 8 months at a time, instead of shorter intervals like he'd been experiencing lately.

Six months ago, he was in California, building a new community with his team. Four months into it, he had to relocate to Texas because one of his employees, Paul Dorsey, had gotten hurt on vacation skiing in Colorado. Being one man down wasn't normally a big deal as they had enough employees to get the job done, but Paul was one of their managers, so Kody needed to step in to oversee a project until Paul came back.

Shortly after Paul returned, Kody got more bad news. Arlo Pereira, an employee at the Georgia location, was resigning. Arlo was moving back to Brazil to take care of his elderly parents that had gotten too sick to take care of themselves.

Kody hated to see him go. Arlo had been an invaluable member of his team for four years, but Kody fully understood the reasoning. Family was important, and he respected Arlo that much more for his decision.

However, it left a spot that needed to be filled, and who better to fill it than the boss himself. Technically speaking, Haven Construction was a company he owned with his cousin and business partner, Jackson Knolls. But the idea to start the company and the type of work they handled was his own.

Kody often thought back and wondered where the time went. What had started out as a small construction company in California ten years ago had grown quite considerably. When Haven Construction first opened its doors, they were a ten-man crew, including the owners, Kody and Jackson, of course, and eight additional men to help them with projects.

Jackson handled most business management tasks like acquiring new business, putting in bids, contracts, etc. While Kody spent more time out in the field, participating in the actual labor and overseeing the team.

Things continued on this way for the first five years of the business, with changes made only to the crew as they had to slowly hire more guys to keep up with the workload.

As the sixth year rolled in, one of their California clients asked if they would be open to building a new single-family home community on the 30 acres of land he owned out in Texas. Accepting the work while simultaneously building new clientele in Texas, work got so busy that Kody and Jackson decided to open a second location.

Two years later, new business was acquired in Georgia while Jackson was visiting Atlanta on vacation. Long story short, after a year of hiring workers temporarily to handle the workload in Georgia, they landed five additional mega-sized contracts that prompted the need for a third location.

Now, with a branch in California, Texas, and Georgia, things were very busy. Each location employed a little over 75 construction workers full-time and had a full team of administrative staff. It seemed the continuous word of mouth from their high-quality work had made the company take leaps and bounds that caused it to quickly expand, and with Kody and Jackson being such sagacious businessmen, they seized every opportunity. As a result, Haven Construction had become very successful.

In addition to the company's success, they'd made investments in stocks and some of the construction properties. They believed it was never smart to keep all of your financial eggs, so to speak, in one basket. Fortunately, that way of thinking paid off for them.

At this point in their lives, both men could easily stop working every day and become the types of CEOs who showed their faces solely to put out fires, sit in on meetings or randomly monitor staff.

But both men loved their work and employees too much to simply become a name behind a desk.

Therefore, Kody and Jackson continued to maintain their respective roles in the company and worked interchangeably whenever the need arose. Kody was no stranger to setting up contracts or taking the occasional business meeting, and Jackson was equally ready to throw on a hard hat and get his hands dirty whenever necessary. They made sure to stay heavily involved with what was happening within the company from day-to-day.

About two years ago, shortly after opening the Georgia location, Jackson decided to relocate from California to Georgia. He wanted to keep an eye on how things were unfolding down there and help the process along. In full transparency, he didn't have to be there. He didn't relocate to Texas when they opened that branch, and he handled most of his business for Haven Construction through email, conference calls and video chats.

In the rare instances face to face meeting were necessary, he could easily catch a flight. His real reason for relocating to Georgia was because he'd met Erica—a sassy, sweet beauty from Jamaica he claimed was the love of his life. They'd gotten married the previous year and couldn't be happier.

The same freedom was afforded to Kody, but like Jackson, he preferred to stay true to his original contributions to the business.

However, now instead of just working in California, he also went to Texas and Georgia as needed. He traveled a great deal more than Jackson because he was single, and it was easy for him to move around. He enjoyed the travel and figured he'd stop doing it whenever it became too much.

He had a condo in California, but he was barely there with how busy things had been with the company. A great deal of the time, he was only there for a couple of hours, it seemed, to change clothes, shower and get some sleep.

When he was in Texas, he either stayed at hotels until the project was complete or stayed inside the actual renovation property if it was a long-term contract, deemed livable and the investor agreed to it. By staying at the renovation home, he was often able to get the work done faster so that the investor could get it sold. He and his crew could work on the home Monday through Friday, and in the evenings or weekends, he would continue work on the house himself, tackling small projects like installing new fixtures or painting.

It just so happened that they'd gotten a new contract for a home renovation in Georgia, with the option to live in. With Arlo no longer on staff and it being Kody's favorite type of construction, he figured why not? Paul was back at work in Texas, and although Kody had been to Georgia a few times for an annual work event and to visit Jackson, of the three locations, he spent less time there.

It would be a nice change to be closer to Jackson again and work on a live-in renovation property. However, he hadn't moved into the contracted property yet. Instead, he was staying at a nearby hotel while they installed a new roof. If he finished the roof by Sunday, he planned to officially move into the property then.

He easily recognized the potential the house had to offer. It was a small ranch style home with three bedrooms and two baths located in a beautiful community in the Atlanta area.

Restaurants, apparel stores, food markets and banks were all within bicycling distance from the neighborhood. He also noticed there was a park, walking trails and a lake nearby.

Kody felt that he was really going to enjoy his time here. The people were hospitable, and the food was delicious. Although he hated eating out so much, as he truly did miss home cooking, it was an unwritten part of the job description that he made the best of.

Currently, he was sitting at a local restaurant called Quaint, waiting to meet with Jackson. They were going to talk over the details of the new property Kody was working on.

Quaint was a nice place that carried a retro vibe that made him think about something you would see on a show like "Happy Days." However, the colors were more vibrant, and the style of decor promoted a more modern edge. It housed gray and gold booths and tables that provided a great view for customers to look out and passersby to look in through the huge windows.

The location-based marketing tactic, rather intentional or not, was good business sense. In front of the building was a busy street and a traffic light. People waiting at the light would undoubtedly look at the restaurant and either get the craving for food or see all the people enjoying themselves inside and want to be a part of the excitement.

A few booths in front of him was a family of four. The man and woman, who he assumed were the mom and dad, were chasing a little girl who looked to be two, around the table. At the same time, the son, who was probably around five or six, stared intently at the colorful images dancing energetically across his tablet screen.

It warmed Kody's heart to see a family together, enjoying one another. He wanted one day to have a family of his own, but he wasn't in a rush. If his parents had taught him anything, it was that good things come to those who wait.

He had been in love once but nothing even close since. It certainly wasn't because he couldn't find anyone. He often approached (or was approached by) women that he didn't mind getting to know. Yet regardless of who approached whom first, for one reason or another, it never panned out.

Maybe he was too picky like all his friends accused him of, but in his mind, most of the women he met just didn't seem to fit. He met a lot of women that aimed to be what they thought he wanted and didn't present him with much of a challenge.

He wanted a woman that had things going for herself and could keep him on his toes. Falling for someone should be fun, enticing and real. So far, it just wasn't in the cards, but that was fine; he was patient. He would find her one day, he had no doubts about it.

Until then, he poured all of his time and passion into his work. He asked himself questions to determine what would make each house stand out from all the rest. For instance, what made things flow better in a home? What was most appealing? What features did families need?

Questions like these sparked a vision of what the completed home should look like. Then he would take care to include those special touches on his projects. Such as a built-in nook for sitting and reading or staring out the window. Mudrooms for families to unload all their outside accessories before entering the home, or a storage closet underneath the staircase. Bottom line, anything that he felt helped to make a house a home.

Every home he worked on brought back memories of how life was growing up with his parents. He was an only child raised by what he liked to think of as the world's best parents.

His mom was a doctor, and his dad was a lawyer. Kids always teased him about his parents being like "The Cosbys", a 1980's TV show, but in reverse.

He didn't mind it, though. He loved his parents, and they gave him a wonderful life. The only thing that would have added the cherry on top would have been having a sibling to share all the great times with.

Luckily for him, where siblings were absent, Jackson was present. They were cousins but acted more like brothers. They were ridiculously close and regularly at one another's house, having fun or fighting. Which, of course, was to be expected of kids growing up.

Even still, despite a few hiccups over some girls, they shared a common liking to in the 8th grade, arguments over sports or random other trivial reasons, they got along great. They enjoyed similar things, and that made for an easier bond. Both Kody and Jackson liked to work with their hands and build.

Unfortunately for Kody's parents, that meant the boys spent a great deal of time around the house breaking things in the name of fixing them.

Kody smiled to himself as he remembered how he and Jackson would shadow his dad, a natural handyman, wherever he went. They wanted to know how everything worked and cornered him with endless questions on the process.

But Kody's dad was a patient man. It was likely from his dad that Kody obtained his naturally calm and relaxed personality. His dad was not at all annoyed by the boys' curiosity. He answered all their questions with care and enjoyment. He even explained the process in great detail and allowed them to perform some of the repairs if the job was simple and safe.

Kody and Jackson were amazed when they helped fix things. They'd run to Mrs. Benton and brag that they did the job on their own with no help from Mr. Benton. Always, she'd laugh and pretend to believe them.

The one difference between the two boys, which turned out to be a benefit, was that in addition to doing repairs, Jackson also enjoyed business. Learning how companies stayed afloat and made their money was an intriguing topic for him. Quite naturally, after college, when Kody presented him with the idea to go into business together, Jackson jumped at the chance.

Kody's parents couldn't have been more proud that their two boys (as they always referred to them) had started a business together. Sadly, a few years after the launch of Haven Construction, Kody lost his parents in a car accident. With Jackson having already lost his parents during his college years, he knew the sadness Kody faced all too well.

Kody's parents were like his own, so their absence didn't leave him unscathed. But as the saying goes, what doesn't kill you only makes you stronger, and their bond was proof of that. The only family they had left was their grandmother, and they made it a point a few times a year to go out and visit her. Not having much family made family a big deal to Kody, and he would do anything for them.

His melancholy thoughts were interrupted by the cook hitting the bell. He was informing the waitress that another order was ready for pickup. Once she retrieved the tray, she turned to look at Kody and gave a flirtatious smile.

Staring intently at him, she made her way to his table. While placing it on the table in front of him, she asked if he needed anything else.

"No, I'm fine. Thank you."

She gently placed a hand on his shoulder in an all too familiar way and said. "If you think of anything, and I do mean anything, just let me know."

Yeah, he knew what she meant alright, but he wasn't taking the bait. Instead, he gave her a responsive nod and left it at that. He was used to women flirting with him. If he were younger, he would have invited her to his place and timed himself on how fast he could have gotten her underneath him.

But now, being 32 and having done a whole lot of living and learning, he was no longer interested in how many notches he could get on his bedpost.

Of course, he still liked sex; he loved it, actually, which was why it was all he cared about for most of his young adulthood. Driving women insane from pleasure, giving them multiple orgasms and even having girls offer to do his work in college because they wanted one night with the talented Kody Benton.

His sexual reputation most certainly preceded him, and he loved it and what it did for his ego. He was probably just as addicted to the praise as the sex itself.

But it got old. It also got complicated because, more often, women would want a relationship, and he didn't. Eventually, when his narrow way of thinking caused him to lose out on someone special, he stopped living his life chasing skirts.

The time had finally come where the adrenaline rush of one night stands or a rotation of "friends with benefits" no longer held his interests. He wanted a woman that could offer him more, and from the obvious "please fuck me" vibes the waitress was giving him, he could tell she wasn't it.

When she stepped out of his line of vision to go check on another table, he saw Jackson standing there smiling way too hard.

"If you need anything, and I do mean anything," Jackson said in a mocking breathy tone.

They both started laughing, and Kody stood up. Pulling his cousin in for a hug.

"If it's not the man himself. How are you, Jackson?"

"I'm pretty good," Jackson said, taking his seat as Kody did the same. "Obviously, not as good as you," he added, nodding in the direction of the waitress.

"Whatever, I'm starving."

"Yeah, I could eat too. I am obsessed with the pastries at this place. I used to come by here a few times a week just to grab one."

"And Erica is ok with that?" Kody asked, giving Jackson an unconvincing look. Jackson had high cholesterol and was supposed to be trying to get it under control. From what Kody knew from their last conversation, Jackson had made some progress in the right direction, but the numbers still weren't in the normal range.

"She isn't, but I don't tell her. Plus, you see that right there," Jackson said, pointing out the window.

Kody looked in the direction he pointed.

"Well, that big building there is called a hospital, and if anything happens, they can fix me up good as new."

"I don't think it's that simple, Jackson, and even though you may be my least favorite cousin, I think I'd like to keep you around."

Jackson smiled, but it didn't quite reach his eyes. Kody's joke made him feel bad about not always taking his cholesterol issues seriously. He was Kody's only cousin, and if something happened to him, he knew Kody would be devastated.

Adopting a more humorless tone, he said, "I know but don't worry. Remember I said I used to come by three times a week, now I'm down to only once a week. Baby steps, little cousin, baby steps."

Jackson regularly referred to Kody as little cousin even though he was only eight months older than Kody. When they were kids, they would fight over Jackson's use of the word "little" when referring to Kody. As they aged, Kody let it go and told Jackson that if he wanted to be known as the one between the two of them that would be arriving at senior status first, he could have it.

But he also realized that Jackson meant it in love. He always tried to protect Kody and look out for him even though Kody had no problems looking out for himself.

"That's what I like to hear," Kody said. Tell me, how is Erica?"

"She's good. She told me to give you a kiss for her, which you know damn well I will not do. But mostly, she sends her love and wants you to know she still hasn't stopped trying to find a woman to marry you off too."

Kody chuckles. "Yup, that's Erica."

Erica was constantly pushing Kody to get married and start a family. At one point, he attempted to appease her by going out on a date with a friend of hers named Michelle, who lived in California. They seemed to hit it off in the beginning, but after a couple of months, it was clear they were not a good match. Michelle was attractive, highly educated, goal-driven and confident.

He loved those things about her, but, at the same time, she was a little too serious for him. Activities such as board games, going bowling or playing laser tag didn't interest her. She more so liked dates that were, as she would call it, "fancy." Activities like couples cooking classes, museums and broadway plays were more her style.

Even though he didn't mind dates like that, he also enjoyed fun. No holds barred, kid at heart, friendly, competitive fun.

Kody and Jackson continued catching up while Kody ate his meal. When he was done, he sat back in the chair, ready to get down to business.

"I'm ready to talk about this new renovation I'm working on," Kody said.

"First, here's your copy of the complete file on the property." Jackson said

He passed Kody a folder with several documents inside. "Of course, I still have to get permits for the additions you want, but that file contains the whole project in a nutshell."

"Great," Kody said, tucking the folder into the work bag he brought in with him. "I'll look over the file later as I already know the basics. Such as the fact that it's a seven-month contract, and he is fine with me living on site during the process. Is there anything else I need to know?"

"Not really. It's pretty straight forward just like all the other renovations we do. I know you've already started work on it. What did you think of it?"

"It's promising. Structurally sound and in a nice neighborhood. According to the report you emailed to me, I see that it was built in the early 50s, and a lot of the features are original to the home. It's going to need the expected things, new windows, roof, flooring, plumbing, etc. Also, I think I will remove some walls to redesign the layout, giving it the more in-demand, open concept look. The good news is, we will be finished with the roof soon and then I think it will be fine for me to move into the house while the crew and I work on the rest."

Jackson gave a sly grin, and Kody knew what was coming next.

"That's good. You've had to do two giant moves these last six months. Sounds like this project would be ideal for you. At least you'd be in the same location for the rest of the year, and who knows, maybe you'll decide to stay permanently."

Jackson was always hinting at Kody spending most of his time in Georgia because he lived there. He knew Jackson missed him and would like to see him more, and Kody felt the same, but he wasn't sure he was ready to stop traveling. He liked working with the different teams and changing up his surroundings.

On the other hand, he had to admit the idea sounded wonderful. Slow down his travel for a while and restore some permanent order to his life. He really should think about it. As for now, he had a hopeful Jackson staring him down. He never liked to just flat out say no to Jackson. So he opted for the easy response and said, "we will see."

Jackson seemed about to say something more but decided against it. He'd broach the subject again soon enough, Kody was sure of it. Instead, Jackson picked up a menu and smiled slyly.

"I think the waitress that's been eyeing you needs an excuse to come over." He raised his hand and said, "Miss, I'm ready to order."

Chapter 4
Winter

Work on Monday morning was exactly as Winter expected, busy. As she pulled in to her reserved parking spot, she saw all the usual foot traffic cluttering the parking lot. The big sign above the building that read "Movie Box Studios" was displayed in tall, bold, yellow letters.

She still remembered how she felt the first time she saw it. Nervous, unsure and thrilled about the possibility of landing her dream job. On the day of her interview, she sat in her car for over thirty minutes, practicing what she would say to the expected questions.

"Why should we hire you? Where do you see yourself in five years? Why did you leave your last position?"

They were all on her list, and she was ready to impress with her well-rehearsed answers. However, Mr. Cordell Sanders, a 65-year-old untraditional, warm, welcoming, downright country boy to the core and the owner of Movie Box Studios, didn't ask her any of that.

Instead, after their initial introduction, he looked at her and said, "Would you like to see a movie?"

She spent the next few hours watching the setting up and filming of movies from various genres. She was so taken by everything as she watched scenes from romance to comedy come to life before her eyes. Somewhere around the seventh setup, Mr. Sanders turned to her and said, "you're hired."

She was shocked. Didn't he need to know things? What if she couldn't meet all the demands he had? Seeing her expression at his offer, he laughed.

"Don't worry, Winter, I looked over your resume, and combine that with the genuine excitement and passion I see in your eyes, you're a perfect fit. You don't need to know everything right off the bat for this position. It's a learn as you go. And from what I can tell about you, you're going to go far."

Surprisingly, he was right. She dove into her new position as a Prop Master and never looked back. She trained with the girl who was the current prop master but was set to leave the company in a few months. She even helped out other departments when she had the time.

Now, seven years later, she still loved this place and all the high energy it brought with it.

Upon entering the building, she was almost knocked over by a person pushing a rack of clothes. At the last minute, she took a step back and thankfully avoided the collision. Yelling on their headset to someone named Terri, they didn't even notice that they almost knocked someone over. She just shook her head and started yet again for her office. About halfway there, her assistant of five years, Lisa Chan, fell into step with her.

Lisa was an Asian woman in her late 20's who was single and had no kids. She was more Americanized than her parents, and she made it known she preferred it that way. She often referred to their way of living as "perfect for them but too old school for her." She was a funny girl, who Winter loved because of the honest and sarcastic tone she brought to the office.

Her humorous personality was actually quite fitting because, minus the glasses, Lisa bore a close resemblance to the famous comedian Ali Wong. Her dry humor was one of the things Winter liked most about her upon their first meeting. Five years later, Winter didn't think she could survive without her amazing assistant.

"How was the wedding? I'm still mad I wasn't able to make it," Lisa said.

"It's fine. Chloe completely understood that someone had to hold down the fort while I was away. I do have tons of pictures I'll be sure to share with you. It turned out just as beautiful and flawless as Chloe hoped for."

"That's nice. Chloe deserves it. Did she enjoy my gift?"

"I'm not sure she even had a chance to look at it yet, but I think it's safe to say a box full of sex gadgets is always a welcomed gift."

"I do aim to please," Lisa said, proud of herself.

"And that you do," Winter responded. "Speaking of, what's going on with the vendor for that horror movie we started last week?"

"You mean the one about the serial killer who keeps killing other people, thinking he is really killing himself each time?"

"Yeah, that one."

"Annoying. Our prop vendor is at it again. He claims that they don't have 20 out of our 30 requested items in stock. He is always pulling this shit. What directive do you want me to take?" Lisa asked excitedly. She loved being able to lay down the law with the vendors.

"Call their main line, using the phone in the back office. The caller ID for it doesn't reflect Movie Box Studios. Ask for Vincent and then ask him about some of those items. If he says they are not available, setup up a phone meeting for me with them at four o'clock. They can't keep pulling this and expect to keep our business. I have four other companies lined up that would be kissing our ass to get the contract to work with us. If Vincent says yes, I still want the meeting, but I'd like to hear from Vincent first."

Shooting Winter a quick glance as they kept up the pace, Lisa asked, "I'm just making sure we are on the same page here. If you plan to do the meeting, anyway, why see what Vincent has to say?"

"Because Vincent is a salesman with loose lips, or at least that's what I have heard about him. He gets paid off commission to get contracts with new companies. Supposedly he holds back inventory items so he can get the contract bonus for signing up a new company. Some say the owner doesn't know this is going on, and others say the owner knows but doesn't care. I need to know if these items are in stock or not, and Vincent is my way to that answer. Also, when I call to end our contract, I plan to mention Vincent if I need to."

"That's what I thought. Ok, I'll get right on it. Anything else you need from me before I go play detective chick?"

"Nope, I think I'm good. Oh, wait," Winter said, stopping and turning to her. "Get me a list of the next ten scenes that need to be…"

"Already completed and on your desk."

"Of course, it is. Have I told you, you are the best assistant in the world today?"

"Nope, but save your words. I like my praises in bonuses."

"Will do," Winter said, entering her office.

She took off her jacket and sat in her chair. As per their conversation, Lisa left the next series of scenes that needed to be prepped on Winter's desk and a bagel from Winter's favorite cafe.

Winter ate the bagel while checking emails. After replying to all the necessary ones, she started creating her checklist for the upcoming scenes. She needed to make sure they had all the requested inventory on time and speak with prop designers for the ones that needed to be altered.

She was at it for hours and had just finished up a list for the sixth scene when an alert popped up on her computer. It read "PATT." It stood for a movie called "Pulling at the Threads."

It was about a quirky guy who finally snaps after he walks in on his wife cheating. He kills the guy in cold blood and then holds his wife hostage in the basement so that she isn't able to tell the police.

Winter didn't often sit in on the scenes, although she was welcome to. However, this movie really piqued her interest. After reading the script and creating the prop list for it, she fell in love.

Today the scene they were filming was the cheating pair having sex—as they were enjoying the aftermath, the husband walks in, sees them in the bed naked and losses his shit.

Winter made it to the area just as filming began. As she watched the intimacy play out for the cameras, she was drawn in. Never in her own life had she ever had sex that ranked anywhere close to the level of what this scene was portraying.

The gasping, the uncontrollable moans and whimpers, it all had to be fake. And not just fake because it was a movie, fake because women didn't respond like that... did they? Her sex with guys was always, what was the word...basic—no fireworks, no uncontrollable screaming and sadly but most shockingly, no orgasms.

The no orgasms part was a total shocker to Jessica and Chloe.

"Never?" she remembered Chloe and Jessica exclaim.

"Yikes," Chloe added with a sad tone. "Maybe your pussy is broken or something."

At the time, she recalls attempting a weak laugh at Chloe's joke meant to lighten the mood, but mostly it just hurt. Not because of the words Chloe said but the fact that it was probably true. Something had to be wrong with her, right? Women didn't just not have orgasms from sex. To date, all of her orgasms came from self-pleasure.

She had tried different positions and, of course, had different partners, still nothing.

The whole thing truly baffled her because it wasn't as if sex itself felt bad. More times than not, the guy would bring her to the edge, or she assumed he did, but her body just never took the leap. Even still, she held out hope that one day it would happen for her. She didn't want to simply believe this was as good as sex was going to get for her.

She resumed watching and enjoying the rest of the scene until she heard someone shout,
"That's a wrap for today."

Winter headed back to her office to pick up where she left off on the scenes list. She had several scenes left, but unlike the first, these wouldn't be simple. She let out a deep breath, typed in her computer password, pulled up her inventory list and got to it.

Around an hour later, Lisa popped her head in and reminded Winter about the 4 o'clock meeting. She also confirmed that per Vincent, the items were available, and he could set them up for an account to start a new contract if she liked. Expectedly Lisa declined, ending the call with promises to think about it.

Winter thanked her for the update and prepared for her call.

The whole meeting only took about twenty minutes, and by the end of it, the owner was very apologetic and promised to deal with the issues. He also offered them a free year of service as a way of apologizing for any inconvenience and in hopes of keeping their business.

Winter accepted the deal but would be looking elsewhere. No way was she staying with a company that had this much drama, but in the meantime, not having to pay a fee would be nice for Movie Box's budget.

She didn't finish with the last scene on her list until 10pm. Afterward, she was so tired she could barely keep her eyes open on the ride home.

The rest of the week was more of the same—late nights and early mornings. She was so glad when Friday came.

She got home, took a shower, and turned on HGTV. It was one of her favorite background noise shows. She didn't have to focus to know what was going on but could always look up and be current on what was going to happen next.

She loved the big reveals. The homes were like Cinderella stories, arriving from rags to riches in a matter of weeks. She sat down with a turkey sandwich and stared at the TV.

Traditional or open concept? That was always the question. And 95% of the time, the answer was the latter. Struggling to keep her eyes open, she waited through all the demolition issues and budget problems for the big reveal. But with the long hours and mental stress of the week, she couldn't keep her eyes open and fell asleep before the glamorous home makeover was uncovered.

Her ringing phone woke her up the next morning.

"Hey, Wint. I'll be there in about an hour," Chloe said on the other end.

Sitting up on the couch, it had totally slipped her mind that weeks before Chloe's wedding, they had planned to spend the day together when Chloe returned from her honeymoon. Her husband, Derek, had an important business meeting in New York that he had to attend, so they'd set up a quick four-day getaway to Jamaica and would do a longer honeymoon later.

"Umm, great. I'll see you then," Winter said as she rushed to get cleaned up and into the kitchen to start breakfast.

When Chloe arrived, Winter had just finished putting their plates on the table. Chloe plopped down in the kitchen chair that was closest to the window and squinted her eyes.

"You forgot, didn't you?"

"No, I… yeah, I forgot," Winter said, abandoning the lie. "How'd you know?"

"Cause your shirt is inside out."

Winter looked down to see that Chloe was right. Taking a seat at the table, she said, "Ugh, I'm sorry, Clo."

"It's fine. I forgot too until I got home after our honeymoon Thursday. I was sad for a little bit because Derek had to leave immediately, but then I remembered I get to spend time with you, and I had something to look forward to."

"Glad I could help. So, tell me, beyond missing Derek, how's married life treating you? Any fun new changes?"

"Not really. Since we were already living together before getting married, nothing much has changed, just my last name. But I will say I love being Mrs. James."

Winter smiled at her friend, and they carried on eating their breakfast with minimal small talk about Chloe's new married status.

The banging on the house next door prompted Chloe to look out the window. Done with their food. Winter got up to put the dishes in the sink and returned to wipe off the kitchen table.

"Oh wow, is someone finally buying the house next door?"

"I'm not sure. I hope so. It would be great to see that house fixed up and have someone permanently live there instead of renters. It's such a nice neighborhood. I hope that a nice family moves in."

"Uh-huh," Chloe said, only half-listening. "That or some sexy single man that can have a warm Winter." Chloe teased.

"You are so silly. I think you have higher hopes for my sex life than I do."

"You're probably right and with good reason, girl. Have you seen all of this visual sexiness laid out next door?"

Chloe was all but glued to Winter's kitchen window.

"Chloe, do you need a leash? You can't be looking at other men; you are newly married."

"I'm married, not dead. My heart may be tied down to Derek, but my eyes are free to roam. I'm just enjoying the view. What's wrong with that? It's like being married to a young sexy Denzel, but you aren't just going to ignore a naked Idris Elba strutting by, are you?"

"I guess not," Winter said, laughing and hitting Chloe with the dishtowel.

"Seriously, girl, come and see the feast for the eyes I'm looking at. Half of them are shirtless, and even their six-packs got sicks pack, Good Lord!"

Winter rolled her eyes and took a glance out of the window. True, those bodies at work were a sight to see. If she hadn't had so much on her mind and been in a different mindset concerning dating or men in general, she might have enjoyed the view a little longer.

"Yeah, they are sexy," she hummed. "But a sexy guy is not at the top of my list right now. Got tons of other things to do."

"Well, you need to pencil that in, sweetie. Didn't you tell me a few weeks ago you were having some plumbing issues? Maybe one of them can plumb *all* your pipes." Chloe said, lifting a suggestive eyebrow.

"You are so bad. And no, thank you, I am good. Yes, it's been a while, but I don't need to pick up random guys."

"Girl, please, you might as well before you become a virgin again."

Shaking her head and pointing a finger at Chloe, Winter said, "Chloe stop it. You're not pimping me out for your entertainment."

"Ok, fine. Let's just talk about something else."

"Finish telling me about the honeymoon. Were you in total bliss the entire time?"

Shifting away from the window to face Winter completely, Chloe placed her hand on her chest, smiled and closed her eyes.

"It was beautiful, Wint. White sandy beaches, beautiful weather, endless drinks, sex until I was dizzy and precious time with my love. I couldn't have asked for anything better."

"Awe, Chloe, that sounds so nice."

"Yeah." Chloe's shoulders slumped, and she looked down at the table. "I never thought I would love a guy as much as I did Reggie, but Derek made his way into my heart.

Reginald, or Reggie as he was referred to, was Chloe's high school sweetheart that she continued to date through college. Everyone was sure they would always be together, but when Reggie got offered an out of state job opportunity and asked Chloe to marry him, she declined.

Although she loved Reggie with all her heart, she simply wasn't ready to be married or leave her family and friends. Sadly, they went their separate ways, and to Winter's knowledge, they hadn't spoken for close to ten years. Chloe was really broken up over him, but eventually, she started dating again, and five years after her breakup with Reggie, she met Derek.

Chloe continued on, "I know after I caught Derek cheating that first year we were together, I couldn't have imagined I would have stayed with him, let alone be married to him. But that was five years ago, and I do love him. He was also very sincere in his apology, and I trust that it won't happen again."

Covering Chloe's hand with her own, Winter said, "I am so happy to hear that. All you can do is follow your heart, and as long as he is making you happy, he can keep both his legs."

They laughed and moved their conversation to the living room. After a few hours of watching movies and having a light lunch, Chloe helped Winter do some sanding on a nightstand she'd found while antique shopping. Winter was planning on restoring it, adding some modern touches, and then donating it to a local women's shelter.

By 9:15, they said their goodbyes, and Winter figured she'd go grab some dinner from a nearby Thai place she loved and then start back working on the nightstand. The restaurant didn't close until 10, so if she left immediately, she should just make it.

She hopped in the car, called to place a pick-up order and arrived ten minutes before they closed. As she walked back to her car through the almost deserted parking lot, her mind was solely on her food. It smelled delicious. The aroma of rice seasoned with bell peppers, basil and onions, were calling out to her. She couldn't wait to get home and devour it.

At her vehicle, she reached in her purse to grab her keys, and a small jolt of pain reminded her of the fall she took last week. It was a lot better and only hurt when she pressed it against something. Taking a second to examine it, everything looked fine; she didn't reopen any of the cuts; she just needed to be careful. Reaching back in her purse, more cautiously this time, she located her keys and pulled them out.

She heard the footsteps behind her only moments before his hand covered her mouth and his knife dug into her throat.

Chapter 5
Winter

Winter was terrified. In her sudden surprise, she dropped the food and gasped. The guy leaned forward towards her ear and, in a low, threatening voice, said, "Remove your purse and slowly pass it back to me."

Winter could feel her racing heart thudding against her chest and a horrified scream clawing at her throat begging to be released. Squeezing her eyes shut, she was able to push it back down. She had to stay calm and think. Using the hand that didn't have her keys, she grabbed her purse and passed it behind to him.

Still not loosening his hold on the cold, sharp blade, he snatched the purse out of her hand. His sudden movement made her jump slightly, but she stiffened again as the pressure of the blade reminded her that her blood could soon be covering the pavement.

Too afraid to swallow or even breathe, she clutched her keys tighter in her hand. She hoped he didn't notice she was still holding them. If she could just stop her thoughts from racing, maybe she could think of a way to use them.

"Easy now, little lady, what's your name?" the man asked in a tone that made her skin crawl.

The pungent smell of alcohol on his breath made her feel sick to her stomach.

"Winter," she said quietly. "Please, don't hurt me. You can take my purse and go on about your business. I won't call the cops or anything." She meant every word. If he left her alone, she would just be thankful to be alive and leave the cops out of it.

Ignoring her request, he said, "Winter? Like the season? Now, that's funny."

He laughed out loud for a few seconds and then abruptly stopped.

"But I must say I've always liked winter." He leaned his body harder against hers and licked the side of her neck. She swallowed hard to keep from screaming or vomiting; at the moment, she wasn't sure which would fight its way out of her mouth first.

"How would you like to turn around real slow and let me get a good look at you, little Winter?"

It wasn't a question, and she knew it. He removed the knife from her throat and then placed the sharp point into her side.

"This is my chance." she thought. There is no way this bastard is going to rub his grimy hands on me. Maybe I can't beat him, but I certainly won't make it easy."

Singling out one key on the ring, she positioned it forward and held it tight. Turning around, she quickly sidestepped to get out of direct range of the knife at her side and then stabbed at his face with the key using all the force she could muster.

Although it was all a blur, she could tell when she made contact. The man screamed, and she heard, rather than saw, what must have been the contents of her purse spill out onto the ground. She hoped like hell he had dropped the knife also.

Not wasting any time, she begin to run.

"You bitch. "I'm going to fucking kill you!" the man yelled.

She only got a few feet before the guy was on her. He was fast. A lot faster than she expected him to be. In one powerful push, he knocked her to the ground and flipped her onto her back. Refusing to give up, Winter fought hard. Punching, kicking and screaming. Some of her blows landed, but it seemed none of them were making an impact; that changed when she struck his face.

Immediately, he started swearing and grunting more death threats.

She tried to hit him in the face again, but obviously knowing what her plans were, he blocked her. She needed to fight harder because he was quickly gaining the upper hand and almost able to cover her mouth and silence her screams. She tried to think, but her mind was blank as her eyes seemed somehow locked in on shadows of the man above her who was moving dangerously fast to control her. This could not be how it ended for her. It just couldn't. Raped or even killed in a parking lot by some perverted asshole.

She kneed him and tried to bite his hand, all the while twisting and turning in an attempt to break his hold and keep him from pinning her down. But it didn't work; he was bigger, stronger and a whole lot angry. Against her best attempts, the man finally managed to completely climb on top of her and successfully cover her mouth.

"You are going to pay for that, you bitch," the guy snarled.

Winter saw his raised fist in the air, and tears began to sting her eyes. There was nothing more she could do. At this point, she could barely move, let alone breathe. She squeezed her eyes shut and tried to brace herself for the impact.

But the hit never came. Instead, the weight of the man was instantly lifted off of her.

She opened her eyes and saw what look to be a tall superhero handling her manic attacker like a rag doll. The man who'd come to her rescue pulled the robber closer to him and punched him in the face. The robber staggered back and spat on the ground.

"Kiss your life goodbye asshole," the attacker said, charging at the guy she now considered her hero.

The robber threw a punch that the hero ducked to avoid. Then, just as quickly, the hero delivered another forceful blow of his own, that landed on the attacker's side. Staggering forward and growling in pain, the robber grabbed at an object on the ground. It was the knife.

Winter saw the glint of it in the shadows as the man began to raise it.

"Watch out! He's got a knife," she yelled.

As the robber sprung forward, with the knife in his hand extended, the hero sidestepped, half turned and then connected his fist with the side of the attacker's face.

Winter heard the knife hit the ground seconds before the guy did. He collapsed to the pavement howling in pain and grasping at the side of his head. He rolled over out of the path of the man towering above him. He clumsily got to his feet, but this time, instead of running toward the man, he turned and ran off.

Winter sat there stunned, staring in the direction of the attacker as he disappeared into bushes. Everything happened so fast she couldn't help but wonder if it was really over? She half expected the attacker to suddenly reappear and come charging again.

She looked up and saw the guy that defended her heading towards her. He stopped in front of her and said something. She just stared at him. She saw his mouth moving, but it was as if her brain couldn't catch up.

She shook her head to clear the fog, and then all sound seemed to flood in.

"Are you ok?" he asked, offering her his hand.

"Yes," she answered shakily as the fear slowly began to retreat. Taking his hand and rising to her feet. She could already tell she was a little sore, but other than that, she figured she was fine. Her mental state was probably way more affected than her physical.

"Thank you so much. It all just happened so fast. I don't know what I would have done if you hadn't shown up."

She was wiping at her clothes and trying to calm her nerves. Now that the immediate danger was over, she feared she might start crying. Not wanting to embarrass herself, she closed her eyes and took a deep breath.

The guy just smiled and tilted her face up. He must have been examining her for wounds, she assumed. That's when she got a good look at him.

"DAMN! He is Gorgeous," she thought. "This man makes the statement "tall, dark and handsome" a mouthwatering reality."

He had broad shoulders and seemed to be almost a foot taller than her. He had a beautiful dark complexion with almond-shaped dark brown eyes that a girl could get lost in. His lips looked soft and inviting, and she found herself wanting to touch them, kiss them, bite them… something.

As he slowly turned her face from one side to the other, she felt her racing pulse calm. The gentle touch of his big strong hands was somehow helping her feel better every second that he remained in contact.

"Perfect," he finally said. And she somehow got the feeling that he was talking about more than her being free of scrapes and bruises.

"I don't see any marks on your face, although this isn't the best lighting. Are you positive you are ok? If you need an ambulance—"

"No," Winter said abruptly. She did not like hospitals and avoided them like the plague. "I'm fine. I think I'm more shaken up than anything else."

"We should at least call the police," he said, pulling out his phone.

"No, seriously, I'm fine. I just want to get home. I don't want to spend all night being asked questions I barely have the answers to. I didn't even get a good look at the guy, and he's gone now," she said, gesturing in the direction the guy had run off.

She looked up at him expecting to see pity, but instead, she was met with compassion and understanding.

"I'm Kody Benton," he said, offering her his hand for the second time that night.

"Winter Daniels," she replied, allowing her hand to slide into his. His already familiar touch was again delicate and careful. She couldn't help but notice how small her hand was inside of his. It was weird, she'd just met him, but he made her feel so comfortable and safe. She didn't want to let his hand go, but needing to clear her thoughts, she slowly withdrew her hand from his.

"It's nice to meet you, Winter. Although I wish It would have been under better circumstances."

"Me too. But…" she shrugged off the rest of her sentence. "Do you live around here?"

"No, I don't. I'm just here for a few months taking care of some things for work."

"Of course, he wasn't local," she thought. "He was extremely handsome, respectful and she was drawn to him. Fate wouldn't be that kind. The guy who'd just basically hit you over the head and run was the local guy!"

"Let me help you get your things," he said.

She turned to see her purse and its contents scattered around. Fortunately for her, her purse was small, and she never carried much in it. She retrieved the small red and gold purse while Kody picked up her wallet, a pack of gum and a tube of lip gloss.

Glancing around for her keys, she spotted them a few feet away. After collecting everything, they walked the few steps towards her car and she noticed her bag of food. She picked it up and placed it in the trashcan. Her appetite was completely gone.

Returning to her car, she looked up at him, and for a moment, they just stared at one another as if they both wanted to say something but couldn't find the words. Being near him helped her to feel less afraid and vulnerable. She didn't want it to end, but she knew it had to. She wanted to get home. She almost wished he could have gone with her, but that was insane. She didn't know this man.

"It looks like I have everything. I wish there was some way I could thank you."

"No thanks needed, Winter. I'm glad I was here." He reached into his pocket, pulled out his wallet and gave her his card. "In case you need anything," he said.

Dammit, even the way he said her name was sexy. She had to get out of there. She took the card and unlocked her door. After she was inside, Kody closed her door and stepped back. She buckled up, turned on the engine and backed out of the parking lot.

As she was driving away, she saw him in her review mirror, heading towards his vehicle.

◆◆◆

By the time she got home, her shaking had returned. In an attempt to calm her body and mind from replaying what she thought were her last moments on earth, she took a long hot shower. When she got out, she made a cup of tea. The combo of the shower and tea did help some, but not completely.

She considered calling Jessica or Chloe but instantly decided against it. She didn't want any pity or consoling. At least not right now because it was so fresh. Speaking about it aloud would only make it all too real once again, and she would probably start crying. She didn't want that.

Then there was Kody, the man that not only rescued her but seemed to draw her in. But just like the thoughts from the attack, she had to push thoughts of him out of her mind too. He'd told her himself, he was only passing through.

She'd done the whole fitting a guy into her life thing through long-distance and never again. Wanting him like crazy or not, she would not be bamboozled by fate or play with fire because that is exactly what Kody Benton was—a sexy, tall, masculine, hard-bodied ball of fire.

She had to stop this! Maybe it was just some twisted complex, like the nightingale effect or hero worship. Her feelings for him was likely solely based on him saving her life. Didn't books say that was a thing? For now, she would just chalk it up to that. Her feelings were just responses to almost dying and being grateful to him.

Then she thought of his lips and how his touch calmed her and knew she was lying to herself. Regardless, she wasn't going to call. She didn't need a man to survive this; she just needed time—time and sleep.

But her solution was short-lived because sleep offered no relief. She tossed and turned all night and kept replaying the assault in her mind.

She abandoned the idea of getting any sleep around 5 a.m. after she had woke for the third time touching her fingers to her neck where just moments ago in the dream the blade had been.

Climbing out of bed, she went to the kitchen and started her coffee maker. While the water was boiling, she went to the living room and switched the TV on. It was still on HGTV, and a home renovation show was just beginning.

The choice between spending the next few hours enjoying one of her favorite shows or going back to bed to battle nightmares was an easy one.
So she spent the next few hours getting lost in home renovation fantasies as a way to escape her scary reality.

◆◆◆

Arriving at work on Monday, she was greeted by the expected hustle and bustle she'd grown accustomed to. Being surrounded by it felt like she was being embraced by a much-needed hug of normalcy from life. Mentally planning out her day, she was approached by Lisa shortly before reaching her office.

"Hey, I wanted you to know that Julius Davenport is waiting in your office."

"Really? Why? I thought his contract was all set, and he'd signed off on it." she said.

Julius was a film director in his late 60's who rented out one of the spaces at Movie Box Studios.

"Beats me," Lisa said with a shrug. "All I know is, he came in this morning and said he had a couple more things to go over and needed to speak with you."

"Alright, thanks."

Upon entering her office, she saw Mr. Davenport sitting in one of her guest chairs, with his legs crossed.

"Good Morning," she said, approaching him with her hand extended. "It's good to see you. Forgive me, but I thought we had finalized everything for your space rental. I hope there aren't any issues?"

"No, no issues at all. I just have a few questions."

"That's fine. Let me grab a copy of your contract." She went to her file cabinet, located his contract and came to sit beside him in the chair that sat adjacent to his.

"Alright, Mr. Davenport, what's your questions?"

"I was wondering how many hours we would have the space for?"

Looking puzzled, she said. "As you can see, your requested time for filming rental is listed on line eight."

"Oh. I see," he said, looking down at the line she was pointing to.

"Well," he said as if in search of something else to say. "How long are the terms for our space rental?"

Now she was completely confused. Not only was he given a copy of the contract, he definitely knew the terms of it. They'd went over it several times in great detail as he was very specific about the timing and amount of space he would need.

"It's right here on line two, you requested fourteen months, and we agreed to the terms for a set price."

"Wow, there it is. For some reason, I guess I thought we had agreed on a shorter period."

"No. Everything was fine with what you needed." Going out on a limb, she asked, "Mr. Davenport is everything ok?"

He looked up at her. "I guess I better stop while I'm ahead since I'm probably making a fool of myself."

"What do you mean?"

"To be honest with you, I wanted to ask you out on a date. I didn't know how to broach the subject, so I came up with this dumb excuse about having some contract issues to discuss."

"Oh wow, Mr. Davenport, I'm flattered. Really, I am, but I don't date my clients."

"I figured as much," he said. "But I had to try. You're a beautiful woman, and I think I'd regret it if I didn't say something. I'm sorry for putting you on the spot."

He was a nice man, and she hated hurting his feeling but her and him… not going to happen.

"No problem," she said. "Please let me know if you have any issues with your contract."

Standing to leave, he said, "I will. You be sure to let me know if your dating rule ever changes."

She smiled, and he left. Sitting at her desk to officially start her day, she looked up as she heard a quick knock on the door. It was Lisa.

"What did Mr. Davenport want? You need me to make changes to anything?"

"No, everything is fine. Actually, he wanted to ask me out on a date."

"Eww," Lisa said, making a sour face. "He's in his 60's and not the good kind."

"The good kind?" Winter asked in confusion.

"You know how some men make aging look like art. They get more sexy and distinguished as they mature? I've seen men in their sixties with bodies like 30-year-olds. Mr. Davenport is the old school looking 60. You can see his age coming from a mile away."

Winter laughed. "He's a sweet old guy; I let him down easy."

Lisa rolled her eyes, "better you than me." Then she started down the hall again.

Shaking her head, Winter logged in to her computer and got to work. All day, on and off, she kept thinking about Kody. Wondering what he was doing. If he was thinking of her or if she should take a chance and call him. Each time she decided that it was for the best that she stay away. She had finally taken a break from dating, and it wouldn't be a smart move to yet again date a guy that already came with a hurdle she'd have to figure out.

She finished up her workday and got home before six. Wanting to keep busy, she got started again on the nightstand she had been sanding. It was going to be a beautiful piece. Sometimes the items she found when she went antiquing she kept after updating them.

Then there were other occasions where she would either sell or donate them. Since she was donating this piece, she wanted it to look extra nice. When she was done sanding it, she planned to paint it grey and add some crystal knobs. She was excited to see it complete and knew the women at the shelter would love it.

She continued working on it a little while longer, and then she called it a night. Eating a plate of leftover spaghetti with two glasses of wine, she slept a whole lot better than she had the night before.

The next morning she felt refreshed. It seemed a long day's work and two glasses of wine did wonders for promoting sleep. Instead of waking up from images of fear from her scary encounter, Winter wished she stayed asleep and enjoyed her explicit sex dream she'd had of Kody.

In the dream, they were back in the parking lot. After a reenactment of the heroic rescue, Kody lifted her up off the ground and started to kiss her. Unable to control the desire they both had, he put her on the hood of her car, ripped off her clothes, and she started helping him unzip his pants. Right before he pulled them down, her alarm went off.

"Fucking Hell!" she shouted when she realized it was a dream.

She stared up at the ceiling, feeling very annoyed that her dreams of Kody were going to have to be nothing more.

Again, she reminded herself that calling him would be a waste of time. Screw attraction or the feeling that he somehow belonged in her life. He wasn't here to stay. Not to mention he was probably already in a relationship. A guy that looked like him had to have a girlfriend or even a wife.

She needed to just let it go and move on. She still had his card but refused to look at it. If she did, her heart and mind would betray her and commit his number to memory, making her attempt to toss the card nothing more than a pointless action.

However, she needed to get rid of it. Grabbing her purse from the nightstand, she blindly reached around in it until she located the thick, squared shape and pulled it out.

Leaving nothing to chance, she closed her eyes and tore it up. Her heart was calling her stupid, but she pushed on. She wasn't going to call him, so why hold on to the card? If she kept it too long, she undoubtedly would have a weak moment and give in. She needed to be smart and protect her heart this time. He was just passing through; surely, if he were meant to be, fate would figure out something else.

She reluctantly got out of bed, walked into the bathroom, flushed the pieces down the toilet because she did not trust putting them in the trash can, and started her day.

It dawned on her that with the pipe issues she'd been having off and on, that flushing a card (even one in tons of tiny pieces) was probably an idiotic move, but the deed was done now. She couldn't take it back. Although a part of her wished she could, she knew it was for the best.

After showering, brushing her teeth and styling her hair in an updo with a few long loose curls left to hang down, she went to the kitchen and started a pot of coffee. Walking into her closet, she took a moment to find something to wear. Deciding on a light gray skirt suit, with a yellow blouse, she began to get dressed. Midway through, her phone rang.

"There is drama on one of the sets. What's your ETA?" Lisa said.

"I'm about to head out in a few minutes." She was buttoning up her shirt and tucking it into her skirt. Grabbing her suit jacket, she asked, "What's wrong?"

"They were filming a bedroom scene with the actor Lance True and the actress Blair Kennedy when one side of the bed collapsed and fell onto Lance's foot. Blair happened to be stretched out on the side of the bed and ended up rolling off and landed on her face. There's already a knot forming on her head. It is crazy in there. I came outside to let you know what was going on."

"Please tell me this isn't the scene with that ridiculous high bed that the director just *had* to have?"

"That's the one. Lance is being cool about the whole thing, but Blair is threatening to sue. I have no idea why. The knot on her head can't make her look any worse; it might even be an improvement."

Winter ignored Lisa's comment about the actresses not so appealing looks and said,
"Dammit. They obviously didn't put the bed together right? Are you able to get back in there to see what else you can overhear?"

"I'll try. Let me call you back."

"Great."

She ended the call, finished getting dressed and abandoned the idea of having a cup of coffee. Reaching for her purse and keys, her phone began to ring again. Assuming it was Lisa, she put it to her ear and said, "how bad is it?"

"Well, we can put that on hold for now. At the moment, there's a fire that needs to be put out."

"Seriously? You mean metaphorically speaking, right?"

"No, there's an actual fire. With all the moving around, some dumb ass knocked over a candle used to help create some ambiance in the scene. Last I saw, that precious bed was going up in flames. Either way, of course, we don't need you to put out the fire; some yummy firemen are coming to do that, but it's a shit storm down here, and Mr. Sanders is having a cow. I just wanted you to have a heads up on the workday fun you are entering into."

Poor Mr. Sanders, he never handled accidents on set well. You'd think he would be used to it by now with so many years in the business, but he just wasn't great at handling catastrophes.

"What in the hell is going on today?"

"Beats me. I'm just here cause you pay me to be."

"I'm glad to see all this mayhem hasn't affected your sense of humor. Be sure to get me the names of those assigned to set up that bed."

"Already did it. I also set up a meeting for you with the two of them. I knew you'd want to speak with them. Would you like two pink slips as well?"

"That won't be necessary, Lisa. Thanks for the heads up. I'll see you soon."

As she was hanging up, her doorbell rang.

"Who could that be?" she wondered.

The last thing she needed to see was some salesman. This day was already turning out highly eventful, and it was still early. It would be great if someone could save her from this mess she was about to walk into at work.

Without even thinking to ask who it was before opening the door, which was a major no-no for her. She swung it open, ready to tell whoever was on the other side that today was not the day. But to her surprise, she opened the door and locked eyes with none other than Kody Benton.

Chapter 6
Winter

Was she dreaming? She had to be. That was the only reason Kody would be standing on her doorstep.

"Kody?" she said, slightly afraid speaking would make him vanish into thin air.

"Winter?" he said, just as surprised.

They said each other's names simultaneously. Then laughed.

"How are you?" she asked

"I'm even better now," he responded with one of the sexiest smiles she had ever seen on a man.

The first time she saw him, she thought he was gorgeous but now seeing him in the daylight was downright sinful, mostly because of all the improper thoughts that were flooding her brain.

He had brown skin that didn't seem to possess even one imperfection. Low cut, wavy black hair with an attractive face that displayed a strong jawline, straight white teeth, warm brown eyes and soft full lips.

She could now see his tall frame and broad shoulders was accompanied by sculpted arms and a defined chest. He was wearing jeans and a white tank top that clung to his body in a way she one day hoped to. He stood there oozing confidence and a natural swag that she was sure made women fall apart everywhere.

He was the type of guy you would see in a magazine, then be compelled to buy said magazine just because he was the perfect visual to pair with your vibrator on a lonely night.

"How are you?" he asked.

"I'm good," she said with a nod.

"Why is he making me so nervous?" she thought.

Aloud she asked, "How'd you find me?"

"I didn't, not knowingly anyway. That part was just massive good luck. I was returning some mail that seemed to—" he broke off. "This is weird, right?"

"I'd say so. You just moved next door?"

"Well, temporarily, yes."

"Oh, so you're renting the place?"

"Not exactly. I'm renovating it so that the investor can sell it. Living there while working on it just speeds up the process."

"That's an impressive way to work," she said. "I'll bet your boss loves that type of dedication."

"Seeing as I am the boss, I would have to agree."

"Impressive," she said.

She couldn't stop staring or smiling. She must've looked like an idiot, but it was hard to believe he was there. She was at a loss for words. There was so much she wanted to say but at the same time awkwardly speechless. She wondered if he felt the same because although he looked more relaxed than she felt, he too was silently staring and smiling.

"I'm sorry I'm staring," he began. "Beyond being totally, albeit pleasantly surprised to see you, I was just caught off guard. Did I catch you heading to work?"

"*Shit, work!*" She completely forgot about the fire she was heading to put out.

"Oh wow. Yes, I am, actually. Emergency down at the office."

She spun around to lock her front door. After securing it, she turned around to face him and saw him extending the mail to her. She pulled it out of his hands, and their fingers touched. Instantly she felt warm all over.

"I hope you have a good day, Winter," he said.

"That voice! Why'd he have to say it so smooth and seductive? He has to know what he is doing. Do I really have to go to work?" she mentally questioned.

"Couldn't I just hang out here, run my fingers up and down that hard sexy chest of his and finish the scene in reality that started in my dreams? Surely they could tend to the fire at work while I tend to the one here."

As if in answer to her question, the phone rang. Pulling it out of her pocket, she glanced at the screen. It was Lisa... again.

"I'm sorry, Kody, I really have to go. But I'll stop by soon so we can talk more," she said.

"Whenever you'd like," she heard him say.

She drove to work in total bliss. She couldn't believe that she had run into him again—the man of her literal dreams. She passed all the familiar scenery on her way to work—the walking trail, the clothing stores and various restaurants.

When she got to the light in front of Quaint, her mouth began to water. She had to stop by and grab some of their delicious pastries soon.

She spared a glance at the mail. Her name wasn't on any of it. It was local ads with her address on it, but the name area simply had "current resident" printed. He really had no chance of knowing it was her. That made her wonder if he thought of her at all since their first encounter. Or did she just become some distant memory pushed aside once he met another beautiful woman?

When she got to work around 9:30. Oddly enough, nothing looked out of sorts or anymore hectic than the normal day-to-day. Walking into her office, she almost ran into Lisa, who was exiting. They both stopped right before colliding.

"Hey, Wint," Lisa said, stepping out of Winter's way. "I was dropping off Mr. Sanders's list of things for you to do as it pertains to this morning's incident."

"Speaking of, what gives? Where's all the chaos?"

"It seems that the assistant director was able to get things under control. Blair is no longer going to sue, at least not anyone within our company, and after they were all patched up, filming for the rest of the week was canceled. The staff plans to reconvene on Monday to decide how to move forward."

Winter sat down in her chair and picked up the list. "At least it's all worked out," she said to Lisa while scanning the document.

Everything on the list was as to be expected. Mr. Sanders always went haywire with wanting her to double, triple and quadruple check setup procedures, staff records and company liabilities when crazy things happened. However, when she got to number four, she was puzzled.

It read: *Gift for niece.*

Looking up, she said, "Is there anything else? I need to go see Mr. Sanders."

"That's it on my end. Catch you later," Lisa said.

Approaching Mr. Sanders's office, Winter could see him sitting at his desk, wearing earphones and completely immersed in his computer. Not wanting to walk into his office without invitation, she knocked on the open door.

Nothing.

She knocked again. This time saying his name also.

Nothing.

She walked in and waved her hand in front of him. Startled, he jumped back, and the force caused the connected earphones to be yanked out of the computer. Putting his hand on his chest, he said, "Damn, Winter, you just about scared the hair off my ass."

She giggled. Mr. Sanders was a country boy through and through. He was always saying off the wall things that sometimes made absolutely no sense but usually got a laugh out of people, anyway.

For instance, when he saw an attractive woman in a magazine, he might say something like, "that girl is so fine, she made my beans sprout out of season" or "if she's digging the dirt, looks like I'm getting buried." He was known for those off the wall statements, and everyone looked forward to them.

"I'm sorry. I tried to get your attention a couple of times."

"It's fine. I was just so taken with this horror scene we filmed a month ago. It's scary as hell, should be a major hit at the box office."

"I'll bet. I don't want to disturb you, I just wanted to ask you about the list you left on my desk. I understand the first three items, but the fourth said something about a gift for your niece?"

"Oh, that. I'm sorry. I added it to the list so I wouldn't forget to ask you. I need your help as I'm no good at shopping. My niece graduates from college soon. I remember when I graduated from college, all excited and terrified but ready to take on the world. The one thing that gave me confidence was knowing that I had people in my corner cheering me on and there for me if I needed them, no matter how big or small. Of course, I'm going to tell her all that, but I want her to have a nice gift that shows, in some measure, how proud I am of her. She's like a daughter to me, and I'll always be there for her. I'm going to see her family in December and would like to take the gift with me. I was hoping you could find me something, and cost isn't an issue."

"I don't know, Mr. Sanders. That's a tall order. What if I don't pick out something that fits what she would like?"

"Trust me, Winter, anything you pick would be 1000% better than what I would think up. You'd be doing me a really big favor."

"I guess so," she said slowly.

"Thank you, and no rush. I don't need it until December 20th."

"Alright, I'll take care of it. If it's something I find online, I'll be sure to forward you the confirmation and order details. Is it ok to have it shipped here?"

"Shipping it here is perfectly fine."

"Ok. If you don't need anything else, I'm going to head back to my office to get some work done before speaking with Brian Dunn and Thomas Stroud about the bed incident this morning. Anything you want to tell me about it?"

"Nothing to add except it was all levels of drama. Hearing the words lawsuit had me so rattled you could have stuck me on the tail of a snake. I haven't gotten a chance to see Thomas Stroud, which I suspect is where the problem lies. Word around the office is that he's been hitting the bottle pretty hard. How he ended up hired, I don't know. I'll have to talk to Helen in HR about that. But I hope I don't see him cause if I do, I'm likely to stick my foot so far up his ass, he'll be shining my shoes every time he brushes his teeth."

Winter hid her laugh by covering her mouth and faking a cough.

"You aren't getting sick, are you, Winter?"

"No," she said, clearing her throat. "Just a little throat tickle, I think."

"Good. Anyway. Let me know how the meeting goes."

"I will," she said, exiting his office.

During her meeting with Brain Dunn, everything seemed to fall in line. He followed protocols as far as Winter could tell and assisted Thomas Stroud in putting together the entire bed.

However, he explained that he handled the screws and bolts for the right side, while Thomas took care of the left, also known as the side that collapsed. She thanked him for meeting with her and told him she would be in touch with him after speaking with Thomas.

Thirty minutes later, Thomas Stroud entered her office. She could smell the faint whiff of alcohol on his breath as they said their hellos, and she told him to take a seat. When he did, he almost instantly seemed to zone out. He was staring straight ahead, looking at the picture of the 1980s filmmaker on the wall as if he had three heads.

"Can you tell me about the incident that happened with the bed this morning?" she asked. "It appears you were one of two people responsible for setting it up."

"Huh," he said with a dazed look in his eyes. "Yes, I sleep in a bed."

"Mr. Stroud. Are you ok? I asked about the bed you handled for setup on stage 12."

"Yes, I set it up. I think it was missing some bolts or something, so I decided to wing it."

"You decided to wing it?" she asked in a what the hell tone. She was really trying to be patient with him. This incident and whatever else he obviously had going on would likely cost him his job.

"Why didn't you notify us of the issue and report that there were missing pieces? I'm sure that you know there are protocols for matters like these."

Thomas was slowly nodding while Winter was speaking, then stopped as his eyes drifted shut. He'd fallen asleep. Right there during the meeting, while she was talking to him!

Annoyed with his blatant incoherence, Winter hit the desk with her hand.

Thomas's eyes popped open, and he jumped out of his seat. "Huh? What? Where am I?" He was looking confused and a bit scared. After a few moments, he seemed to settle and sat back in the chair.

"Mr. Stroud, have you been drinking, or have you taken something?"

"I had a few beers before work but no more than three because I have control." Then he looked up and off to the side and said, "Or was it four?"

Winter was pissed at not only his disrespect but his negligence. This whole thing could have easily been avoided if he were professional on the job. She wasn't sure who hired him or how he'd been at the company this long with his clear issues with alcohol/substance abuse, but she was ending it.

As Thomas appeared to be falling asleep yet again, she picked up her phone to reach Lisa. She would order him a taxi to make sure he got home safely, but his time of employment at Movie Box Studios was over. When Lisa answered, Winter said, "looks like I'll be needing that slip after all."

"I'm on it!" Lisa said, a little too excited.

◆◆◆

"We have to stop meeting this way, Miss Daniels," Kody said when she opened the door.

It was two days later, and he was once again on her doorstep offering her another tiny pile of misdelivered mail. He was so handsome and mesmerizing. Looking at his face was truly the perfect way for her to start her day. He was sporting a white tank, jeans and a sexy smile.

"I hope I didn't catch you in a rush again?"

"No rush today. I'm sorry about that, by the way. I'm a Prop Master for a film studio, and we had a major mishap on set. My assistant was keeping me up-to-date as things unfolded, but luckily no fires to put out this time," she said.

"Unless you are counting the one between my legs," she thought.

"The movies, huh? Must be exciting to see everything come together, or in your case, being the one to *put* everything together."

"It is. It's my dream job. Fun and fast-paced, but I like the challenge."

She saw a look of something flash in his eyes, but it was gone before she could register it.

"We all like challenges," he said, smiling.

"That damn smile. Should I just give him my panties now?"

"I wonder if our mailman has been drinking or something. Two times in one week," she said, taking the mail from his hands. She tried to avoid touching his fingers because even the slightest touch from him did something to her.

"Could be, he said, letting go of the mail.

"Regardless, I'm glad you stopped by. I wanted to see you before I left for work yesterday, but I saw you talking to a guy in a suit and thought it might be rude to interrupt."

"That was the investor. He wanted to see what we'd done so far. Any particular reason you wanted to see me? Although you never need one," he said.

"To fuck your brains out," she thought before she knew it.

"I wanted to give you a proper thanks and invite you to dinner. You know, for saving my life and all."

Then feeling the need to explain more, she continued, "I should have offered the first time you stopped by, but I guess I was a little thrown. Anyway, it's a friendly dinner, nothing extreme or fancy. You can even bring your girl."

The last part about him bringing his girl just kinda fell out. She was nervous. She didn't want to be coming on to him and find out she was making an idiot of herself. Wait, she shouldn't be coming on to him at all. She was taking a break; dammit, a break. Why didn't her heart and body understand that!

Cutting into her mentally berating herself was Kody chuckling to himself.

"The only girl in my life is my grandmother. She is as sweet as she wants to be but doesn't get out much. I'm sure she would appreciate the invitation but unfortunately wouldn't be able to make it."

Slightly embarrassed, Winter looked down for a brief moment. "Sorry for assuming, So dinner tomorrow night at six?"

"I'd love that," he said.

Chapter 7
Kody

As Kody walked the short distance next door, he was smiling to himself. He was aware of the effect he had on most women, and he was happy to see that Winter wasn't immune.

Her attraction to him made her nervous, and he liked that. Not because he wanted to make her uncomfortable in any way, but he knew that it meant she liked him a lot. And liking him meant that she would have trouble staying away from him. Which worked out great for him because he wanted to know everything about her.

She was beautiful and courageous, and he had to know more. The night they met, he noticed a strong attraction to her that he knew she'd felt as well.

Thinking back to seeing her fight for her life, and losing at rapid speeds, he could feel the anger in him began to resurface. If he wasn't so familiar with self-control, thanks to his dad and grandfather, he probably would have killed that piece of shit. God knows he wanted to.

Being a black belt in karate did have its perks, but he always had to be careful. The threat level from that asshole was minimal at best, and with Kody's size and frame, self-defense to the extent of seriously harming the guy or worse, would be questionable.

Thankfully he was picking up dinner when he did. He was working in the house and had lost track of time. He'd made it back to his truck and was just about to close the door when he heard a muffled scream.

Although the parking lot was pretty empty, it was easy to miss them because they were on the ground. Heavy brush and another parked car had totally obscured their scuffle. The thought that he could have lost her before even having the chance to know her started a fresh wave of anger.

Then, remembering her face looking up at him, safe and alive, made him shift his focus.

After she had left, he got in his truck and just sat there. Their brief encounter had affected him in ways he hadn't felt in a long time. He didn't know if he'd see her again. He gave her his number because he had to try to keep the lines of communication open, but he didn't want to be pushy.

She'd already had a horrible night. What type of asshole would he be if, after a guy physically hit on her, he did the same metaphorically?

Normally he was very upfront about what was on his mind. He didn't like beating around the bush or playing games, but as hard as it was to let her leave and place the ball in her court, he'd done it.

He really hoped she'd call. He wanted to hear her voice and feel her hand in his. She was perfect. Probably around 5'4", slim body, enticing curves and long black curly hair. Her chocolate complexion and beautiful smile made him want to kiss her lips and then everywhere else. She had nice size breast that he was sure would fit perfectly in his hands and an ass that made him daydream about bending her over.

Yes, he'd remembered every detail of that gorgeous face and body, and the sexual attraction was evident, but it was more than that.

He worried about her. Wanted to know that she was truly ok after everything. And thanks to fate, he no longer had to wonder. He would be living next door to her for the next seven months, and that was a very good thing. The ball was now back in his court. And although he'd take his time and try not to press her too much. He would get his time with her. He had to. He liked her too much.

He'd even already told Jackson about her. Well, about their encounter anyway. The next morning after the incident, he was having a phone meeting with his cousin about all of his plans for the current renovation.

Once they had things squared away and Jackson asked him what else was new, he told him about the attack the night before.

"Please tell me you handed him his ass, little cousin?" Jackson had said.

"You know I did," Kody said.

"I don't doubt it. I've seen you in action, and I'm sure the asshat didn't wake up feeling too good the next morning. Which is better than that piece of shit deserved."

"My sentiments exactly," Kody agreed.

One major pet peeve that Kody and Jackson shared was men's abuse toward women.

During their senior year of high school, a girl named Sherri Cooper was dating one of their football team members, Dean Russo. Dean was a cool guy most of the time, but everyone knew he had a temper. One time after their team had lost a football game, Dean was highly upset.

His sour mood escalated when he was ready to leave and Sherri still hadn't made it to the car. She was a cheerleader and got held up by friends while returning some of her gear to the locker room.

When she got to the parking lot, Dean was leaning against his car with two of his team members. As the story goes, she tried to explain to Dean why she was late and kept apologizing for delaying him, but he wasn't really interested in her apology.

Finally, she said to him, "let's just go home. You'll feel better tomorrow," and then walked away. He took that as her disrespecting him in front of his friends and started hitting her. The two coward team members who basically worshipped Dean didn't jump in to stop it. They were likely afraid Dean would beat their asses too.

But after hearing the commotion from a few cars down, Jackson was glad to give Dean a taste of his own medicine.

He ended up breaking Dean's nose and might have done worse if Kody didn't arrive in time and stopped him.

It was the talk of the school for weeks because a few people saw what happened and told others, but no one that mattered was saying a word. Dean was afraid Jackson would get his hands on him again, and Sherri was too embarrassed. Dean's two idiot friends were scared enough of Dean; they most certainly didn't want to piss off Jackson.

When the principal confronted Jackson about the rumors going around the school and his part in the fight, he denied it.

Feeling that Dean got exactly what he deserved, Kody vouched for Jackson, saying that they left the game shortly after it ended and had no idea what everyone was talking about. However, he did see some guys from the other school having a heated conversation with Dean, so maybe that escalated to the fight that the principal had heard of.

With no evidence to do anything more, the principal let it go. Sherri, of course, broke up with Dean, and Dean stayed under the radar the rest of the school year. That was a memory that Jackson and Kody fondly remember because neither of them liked Dean. The only problem Kody had was that he didn't get to punch Dean himself.

He felt his phone vibrate in his pocket.

He pulled it out and checked the display that read Jason Pugh. Jason was his project lead in California.

"Hey, Jason, How are you?" Kody said.

"Busy as hell. How are things down there in Georgia?"

"Very good, the house we are renovating is in a nice area, and I've got big plans for it."

"You always do. I know how much you love renovations. Listen, I don't want to keep you, but you know Mrs. Dorsey, the 78-year-old widow that stays in the community we do the free work in?

"The one that always tries to pay us in knitted blankets?"

"That's the one. Her house has a leak on the roof. I was doing some work in one of the other houses in the community, and I stopped by to check on her, and she showed it to me. I can repair it by replacing a few shingles, but the whole thing looks kinda bad. How do you want me to handle it?"

Kody thought a minute. Then said, "just replace the whole roof. Get Austin to give you a hand. He is really good with roof work. Write up the invoice and mark it paid like we do the others. The accountant will know how to handle it from there."

"Alright, Boss. Anything else you need on my end?"

"Yeah, stop calling me Boss."

"Sure thing, Boss," Jason said and ended the call.

Kody shook his head and placed his phone back in his pocket. He never liked being referred to that way, and his team knew it. Years back, when they'd started working together, he told them calling him Kody would be fine, that it was even preferred, but every so often when a new guy started, they would reference him that way.

The old guys would correct the new guys, but it kept happening. Eventually, it became a running joke that Kody took in good spirits.

Taking out his trim removal tool, Kody started loosening one of the original windows in the living room. This house was small, but it had a lot of windows. The good thing about that was that it gave the house tons of natural light. He decided to replace the old windows with new ones that didn't have grids. Windows with grids carried a more traditional look. Replacing them with gridless windows would produce the more modern look the investor wanted for the home.

Coming up behind him was one of his team members, Gus.

"I saw you talking to the lady next door, and you haven't stopped smiling since. Did you get her phone number or something?"

"Something like that," Kody said, his smile reappearing.

"Well, I've seen her a few times, and she is one sexy woman. If you don't ask her out, I will. Besides, she might not go for the whole tall, nicely toned body type; my style may be more to her liking," he said, patting his beer belly with a laugh.

"I'll be sure to let her know you're available, Gus."

Kody got back started on the window. He made a mental checklist of things that he would need to replace in the kitchen. He'd been looking at some designs from the previous kitchen remodels he'd done, and there was one in particular that he thought would work perfectly and make great use of the space.

Plans for the kitchen reminded him that he would need to decide on dinner for the night. He could grab a salad from one of the local restaurants or go by the grocery store and buy a few ready-made items from the deli area. He wouldn't be starting work on the kitchen for a few days, so he could store a couple of salads in there to give him a break from eating so much fast food.

Even though he would be staying in the property for seven months, he didn't like to buy a lot of groceries. In no form or fashion did he ever get so comfortable in the renovation properties that he treated them like his own home. If he did, it would mean they had more stuff to move around when they started doing work in that area.

But even though he only kept the bare minimum in the fridge, a few salads might be a good idea. It made him wonder what Winter had planned for dinner tomorrow. Would she buy something or cook a meal? Then he wondered if she knew how to cook.

As if that really mattered. The food could taste like burnt gravel, and he'd still eat it happily. Yup, he may not have known what he was in for, but he knew what he wanted out of it… her.

Chapter 8
Winter

She woke up Friday morning nightmare free and practically floating on a cloud. Today was the day—dinner with that gorgeous man, Kody. Getting out of bed, she wondered what she should cook and wear.

As far as food went, she thought maybe an Italian chicken pasta, cooked in a white wine sauce would be nice. Maybe it would have been smart to ask him if he had any requests, but that thought didn't dawn on her until now.

Considering her next decision, she thought about her wardrobe. Unlike the idea of a meal, the choice didn't seem to come as easy. She wanted her outfit to walk that fine line between slutty and classy. Just because she wasn't going to have sex with him didn't mean she didn't want to turn him on.

"Had it really been over a year since she last had sex?" she thought.

Normally that didn't bother her so much, but to be fair, her life usually didn't consist of a Kody.

The thought made her giddy. She had never been so ready to get her workday started, so she could end it. Mental images of his handsome face called to her, and she couldn't wait to see him. Opening the shower curtain and reaching for the knob, she turned it on and… nothing.

"Oh no, not this again."

She turned the knob into the off position and back on, again nothing.

Assuming the third time was the charm, she made a final attempt, only to get the same result. She had been having problems with the water on and off for a few months now.

It was either running with low pressure or it would stall and take a few moments to come out. She kept meaning to get a plumber to take a look at it, but it would suddenly start working fine, and all over again, she would forget about it.

"Think, Winter, think," she said aloud.

She had to get ready for work. Checking the water in the guest bathroom didn't provide any good news, as it too was out of commission. She was, however, surprised that the water in the kitchen sink worked.

At least she could brush her teeth and wash her face, but unless her idea of showering was standing in front of the kitchen sink with a bucket, she needed to figure out something else.

She could call in to work and spend the day looking for a plumber, but that would mean some important last-minute projects wouldn't get finalized. Chloe lived on the way and normally didn't go into work until around 10am; maybe she could stop by there and shower before heading in. She picked up her phone to call Chloe.

"Hey, Wint," Chloe answered.

"Hey, Clo, can I stop by and shower really quick before work?"

"Sure. Everything ok?"

"Got an issue with my stupid pipes."

"No comment," Chloe said.

Winter laughed. "Get your head out of the gutter. I mean my literal pipes. You know, the ones in the wall?"

"If you say so. You know you are always welcome to use my shower anytime, no questions asked."

"Thanks."

After a brief stop at Chloe's, Winter arrived at work only a little late. After tying up a few loose ends for filming projects, she moved on to search for a plumber that could come out on short notice. She had no luck. None of the companies in the area were any help. The earliest one said they could get someone out was Tuesday. It was Friday, that was four days away! She thanked them and hung up.

She figured she would ask around at work first. If no one knew of anyone that could come out sooner. She'd call the company back and accept the Tuesday availability. She would also call off work Monday and Tuesday and put that bucket and rag to good use in front of the sink.

She knew Chloe would tell her she could come by again, but she didn't want to impose. Chloe was a newlywed, and they needed their space. One favor was enough. Even if Chloe wasn't married, Winter didn't like to repeatedly cash in on the kindness of those around her.

Decision made, she jumped back into work, and the day flew by. By the end of it, she had finished setting up all the new contracts that were open on her calendar and lent a hand setting up scenes. It seemed everything had been dealt with as it pertained to work, but her personal issues still needed solving.

No one knew of a plumber that was available any sooner. Therefore, defeated and exhausted, she had to call the company back and accept the Tuesday appointment.

Wanting nothing more but this day from hell to be over, she headed home around 5pm. She felt like, for some reason, she woke up in a good mood, but that good mood now seemed millions of years ago. She couldn't even remember what she was happy about because she was starting to get a headache on top of everything else. That's when it dawned on her she hadn't eaten all day. Not wanting to make any stops, finding food at home won out easily.

When she got there, she hadn't been inside longer than ten minutes when the doorbell rang. She looked at the clock on the wall; it read 5:57.

"Who could that be?" She thought as she headed to the door.

She opened it to see Kody standing there.

Face palming and shaking her head, she said, "Oh goodness, Kody, I completely forgot about dinner."

"No problem, is everything ok?"

"No, it isn't. My water stopped working in both bathrooms this morning, and I haven't had any luck finding someone to fix it. I may have to reschedule our dinner."

"Do you mind if I take a look at it?"

Winter's brows knitted together. "You're a plumber?"

"Amongst other things," he said. "I'm a contractor with an extensive background in all things home related. I can basically build a home from the ground up."

Damn. Good looks and deep knowledge. Winter had to remind herself to slow down. He was very appealing, but he was temporary here, so she needed to keep her cool.

"If it's not too much trouble, I'd really appreciate it? Come in."

Kody stepped over the threshold and into the entryway. "You have a beautiful home," he said. "How long have you been here?"

"Thanks. About four years, " Winter answered.

"Nice. I assume the bathroom is straight ahead on the left?"

Puzzled, she began, "How did you…" then stopped. "Oh yeah, you are living in a similar model next door. Well, have at it," she said, stepping aside and gesturing towards the bathroom.

With a nod, Kody headed toward the bathroom.

Winter watched him walk away. He was wearing a black and gray shirt with dark jeans and smelled amazing. She, on the other hand, was still wearing her work suit, minus the matching jacket. She glanced at her reflection in the decorative mirror she had in the entryway.

She didn't look too bad. It wasn't the look she had planned this morning, but with all things concerned after a long day's work, she could have looked worse. Thankfully her hair was still neat, and the skirt and blouse she wore gave her the appearance of having it together, even though at the moment she really didn't.

She went to what she considered her kitchen/dining room table and sat down. Her place was so small, she actually didn't have a dining room. Her kitchen and living room basically shared a space, separated by her kitchen island. But she didn't mind; in fact, she loved it. She was a single woman with no kids, so it was big enough for her.

"Is today the first day you had problems with the water?" Kody asked from the bathroom.

"No. I've been having problems for months now. The water pressure has seemed to be getting weaker."

"Makes sense," he said.

"If you don't mind me asking, where are you from?" she asked.

"I'm originally from New York, but we moved to California when I was about five.
What about you?"

"I'm from here," she said. "Born and raised in Atlanta."

"One of those original peaches they talk about," he said.

She smiled as her mind took her to naughty places.

"Yeah, I guess I am," she said.

"How long will you be working on the house next door?"

He didn't answer, so she figured he probably didn't hear her. She heard stuff being moved around in the bathroom and assumed he was trying to get to the valves under the sink.

After a few minutes, she heard him approaching the living room area.

"You mind if I check the kitchen faucet?" he asked.

"Be my guest."

He entered the kitchen and turned the water on in the sink. She could hear the gentle splash as it came out, without much force behind it. Next, she heard him open the cabinet doors under the sink as they gave a light squeak of protest.

After another moment, he walked in and pulled out a chair to sit down and join her.

"Ok. How bad is it?" Should I just toss the whole house now?" She felt so stressed. The cost of repairing this would likely be astronomical. She should have gotten someone out to fix this months ago.

"Not the whole house. I think it still has a few years left in it," he said.

"Alright, what's the repair estimate?"

In response, he said, "Pass me that notepad and pen, please."

Giving him the requested items, he took a moment, wrote something, tore it out, folded the paper, then slide the sheet across the table to her.

She looked down at it, amused. Picking it up, she opened the paper and smiled. It was the number seven.

Smiling, she said, "Two things. First, what's with the dramatic note?

"It got you to smile, didn't it? You've been looking stressed since I got here. Plus, since you work in film, I assumed you could appreciate the theatrics."

"You thought right. Now on to the second." Turning the paper toward him, she said, "what's with the seven?"

"It stands for seven months. You asked me how long I'd be here. I'm here until mid-March."

She nodded. It was now late August, merely days away from September. His timeline was definitely a reminder to avoid entertaining the notion of getting too close to him. He would be gone soon enough. If she could just keep that in the forefront of her mind, she would be ok.

Putting on her best business face, she said, "Thanks for trying to soften the blow, I really appreciate it, but you never answered the question about costs."

Noticing her shift in demeanor, Kody said, "You have galvanized pipes and low to non-existent water pressure throughout the house. This indicates corrosion in the pipes. It's currently only affecting both bathrooms, but in time it will affect the whole house. Repairs for just the two bathrooms cost somewhere between four to six thousand dollars, while a total home repair is approximately ten thousand."

Winter's shoulders slumped, and her attempt at keeping a business-like edge got traded in for her earlier response... face palming. This was a nightmare. She had some money saved but fixing the two bathrooms would clear that out, and she couldn't even think about fixing the whole house. She'd have to get a loan for the rest, and she didn't like loans.

She felt him gently touch her hand, and she looked up.

"Oh, I'm sorry," she said. "I'll just need a couple of hours to think about which route I'd..."

"It's going to be ok," he said, cutting her off before she could further explain. "I'll do the work, and I won't charge you for it."

"What in the hell!" she thought. "Was he just pulling my leg? Or flirting with me? There are definitely less expensive ways to flirt."

"You're joking, right?" she said to him.

He looked at her with a straight face, "why would I be joking?"

"If he isn't joking, what type of game is he playing?" Winter wondered. "No one did anything for free. Especially not home repair work! Either he thinks I'm some damsel in distress who can't pay her own way, or he wants me to owe him a debt.

Maybe it was a bit of both, but I am not some weak woman; I can fix this. And as for him thinking he can get me to owe him sex in exchange for service, he is so right...WRONG, I meant wrong!" she mentally yelled at her body to get with the program.

She was not going to exchange sex for pipe work! Yes, he was fine, downright gorgeous even, but she was not an idiot and didn't like the idea of being indebted to him.

Then again, she'd have to wait until next week for a plumber, and why wait when there was a plumber sitting right there? But she couldn't let him do it for free; that added too many complications to the matter.

Realizing she had been silent way too long, she said, "Because no one does anything for free."

"Now, you've met someone that does."

"I don't believe you."

He laughed. It was a nice laugh, one that helped ease some of her apprehension.
"Come on. Seriously I don't mind. I'd love to work on the house, and did I mention I could start as early as tomorrow?"

It may have been her empty stomach making her crazy, but he really did sound serious. But why? He'd already done enough.

"Really tomorrow? Don't you have your own projects to tend to?"

"Usually, I don't do much work on the weekends. If I must, I do small things on the inside of the home like install light fixtures or replace outlet covers, but I try to stay away from the larger projects."

"Now that just makes it sounds like I would be working you for nothing on your off days. I don't think that would be a good idea. I don't like feeling like I'm indebted to someone, so just make me a fair offer, and you're hired."

His eyes wandered to the corner of the room where she had a huge blue and gold abstract painting, with dashes of white lines throughout. It was simple but elegant and went nicely with the overall room decor.

He noticed a large fluffy white rug that lay in front of her couch and expanded out to about 30 inches in front of the fireplace—the things he could do to her on that. He imagined pulling her clothes off and spending hours driving her insane from pleasure.

"One day," he thought to himself, "One day."

His eyes continued to scan the room for a few seconds longer, then finally they were back to her.

"Tell me, Winter, what do you think about non-monetary payments?"

"I knew it! He thinks I am some dumb woman who would easily jump into bed with him out of desperation for her situation. Well, he is wrong." she thought.

"Listen, I don't know what you think—"

He chuckled and interjected, "I was talking about food, Winter."

"Food?" She said as confusion halted her thoughts.

"Yeah. For instance, what were you planning on making tonight? I mean before the whole plumbing debacle."

"I was going to make an Italian chicken pasta, cooked in a white wine sauce."

He closed his eyes and exhaled.

"I love Italian food. I think that would be a fair trade. You cook dinner for me, let's say once a week until the job is done, and we will call it even."

"How long will the work take?"

"About a week. That would include drywall repairs and painting. But since I am only working on the weekends, it would take a month."

She thought about it. One meal per week, for one month, was four meals. That was nothing—four meals for a ten thousand dollar job!

"Kody, I truly appreciate the obvious faith you must have in my cooking, and while I do agree that I'm a pretty good cook, my skills in the kitchen are not up to par for a ten thousand dollar trade."

"Isn't that my choice to make?" he asked.

"Are you sure? That's a lot of money you're missing out on."

"Winter," he said in a way that somehow came off as caring and firm at the same time.

"I'm good on money; what I don't have is home-cooked meals, which I miss because I don't have the time to do it myself. You have a problem, and I have the solution. But since you are so determined to debate this, let me just end it now. Didn't you say you owed me for saving your life?" He looked at her with a checkmate smile.

"Dammit," she thought. "Why'd he have to pull the "I saved your life" card? Of course, I can't say no after that. Plus, he really does seem sincere. And what was that comment about not needing money, who didn't need money? Just how much money does he have?"

Deciding it was none of her business, she said, "How does dinner on Sundays around seven sound?"

"Sounds good to me."

"Any menu requests?"

"Surprise me."

"Alright, if you say so."

"I do. Speaking of food, since we had to cancel dinner would you like to order pizza?" he asked.

Feeling her stomach almost jump for joy after being unintentionally ignored all day. She picked up the phone and asked, "Are you fine with meat lovers?"

Chapter 9
Winter

While waiting for the pizza, they made small chit chat. Even though they had already seen each other several times, they still hadn't had proper introductions.

She told him all the general stuff about herself, such as how she spent most of her time, either working or with her close friends, background information about her life growing up, where she went to school and how she got started on her chosen career path.

She even told him about how unknowingly close he was to being murdered by her, the day he woke her up banging on the roof the morning after Chloe's wedding. He got a kick out of that little story and told her he would have loved to see her stomp over there, all angry and yelling at them. According to him, it would have been adorable.

It was nice talking to him. He listened, commented and asked questions of his own while supplying answers to the same questions on his account. She really liked him and couldn't believe he was single. There had to be a catch; there just had to be.

This guy was 32, no kids, from a well to do family and owned a very successful business. They even had tons in common; their parents were deceased, they both had no siblings and enjoyed many of the same hobbies. Without much effort, the conversation just flowed.

"Yeah," she thought, "He probably has some serious skeletons in his closet."

As great as the getting to know you was, it seemed they both were steering clear of the elephant in the room—the horrible experience that brought them together in the first place... the attack. It was still a much too close memory that she hadn't mentioned to anyone. She was thankful when the doorbell rang because she was able to dodge the topic a bit longer.

After grabbing the plates, glasses and sitting down at the table, Kody said, "So how are you?"

"Oh, I'm fine. My plumbing drama will be solved, thanks to you, and I met all of my deadlines at work. Life is good."

"That's not what I meant," he said, studying her.

She knew that wasn't what he meant; she could hear it in his tone. He wanted to know about her mental state since the attack.

"I'm fine for the most part. Sometimes sleeping can be a challenge, but the past few nights, no issues."

He could tell she didn't want to talk about it, but he had to at least make sure she knew he was there if she needed him.

"If you ever need me, I'm only a call away, Winter."

She looked down to avoid his eyes. She was touched by his concern; although she knew she had no reason to be, she felt slightly embarrassed.

"Umm, about that, I don't have your card anymore. I seemed to have accidentally thrown it away."

"Accidentally, huh?"

"Yeah," she said. That was her story, and she was sticking to it.

Noticing her phone lying on the table, he pushed it closer to her and said, "Maybe we will store it here this time, you know so that you don't accidentally throw it away."

"Good idea," she said, picking up the phone and entering his contact info as he rattled it off for her.

Attempting to get out of the conversational spotlight, she asked, "Where'd you learn those smooth moves the night of the attack. You some famous martial artist or something?"

Kody began tracing his finger around the rim of his cup.

"Yeah, something like that. Just without the famous part. My grandfather was in the service. During his stay in Japan, he developed a major interest in Karate. He studied hard and became a black belt. He even won a few local tournaments. He continued his practice when he came back home to the States, and eventually, when he had his son, he passed it down to him, and long story short, my dad passed it down to me. I started training when I was five. Both of them always stressed that it was less about the actual fight and more about your mental control. Being able to center yourself amid chaos and think clearly will make a bigger impact when you find yourself in dangerous situations."

"Lucky for me then," she said more to herself than him.

It might be a good idea for her to ask him to teach her some of those moves because she was clearly an easy target. However, she didn't want to talk anymore about the experience, so she decided she'd ask at another time.

"Tell me more about your job, I know you love it, but what exactly does a Prop Master do?" he asked.

She was relieved at this change in the subject.

"In a nutshell, I break down scripts to determine what props will be needed for the various scenes throughout the movie. I'm responsible for the procurement, inventory, care and maintenance of all props associated with productions and ensuring that they are available on time and fall within budgetary requirements. I also set up meetings with new clients to get contracts for them to rent out spaces in the studio."

"Sounds like a lot of work."

"It can be, which is why I have an amazing assistant. There is also a team dedicated to handling the setup of the scenes. When I'm not busy creating the lists, reading scripts or researching props, I help out with that part too."

"A woman with many talents. I like that. And according to what you said the other day, there is also a lot of unfortunate accidents?"

"Sadly, sometimes there are. The most recent was a bed falling apart during filming, and the actors got injured. We don't always use real items, but depending on the scene, sometimes we have to, and in this case, it didn't work out so well. There was also another instance where a dog who had a crazy case of diarrhea…"

As she told him about the funny, scary and shocking situations that took place on set, he hung on every word, watching her animated hand movements and her eyes light up as she spoke of the job she loved.

"What about you?" she said when she was finally done. "Tell me more about the renovation projects. How exactly does that work? It must be tough living in a reno. I love watching HGTV and people always say that it's a nightmare."

"It's not so bad. I don't have as much stuff as a person that actually lives at the house. Plus, I don't stay in a lot of my projects, only very select ones owned by investors. It has to be in the contract that they are fine with me living there while working because obviously, they have to keep the power on. Also, there have to be working appliances in the home, and there can't be any safety issues like mold or damage to the foundations. To make a long story short, the homes I stay in generally can be sold as is, but to get top dollar, the owner/investor would rather it be updated and repairs made."

"Ok, so basically, you can live in the house like normal for the contracted time?"

"I can, but I try to keep a small footprint. For example, I only move a bed and a dresser into the house. Nothing more like sofas or TVs. I like to keep the areas as clear as possible because we need to work around anything that I bring in. I also rarely, if ever, touch the stove, and I only keep the bare minimum in the fridge."

"Wow. I think that would be hard for me?"

"For some people, it would. I get that, but I'm on a project to work, so I don't require much."

"Is there seven months of necessary work in that house? Is it that bad?"

"No. For the age of the home, it's actually in pretty good condition. Any updates or repairs I have planned can be completed within 4 or 5 months, but my cousin always overestimates the contracts because of permits. With this home, I am going to tear down some walls and extend the master bath. Sometimes, waiting on the all clear before we can continue working can mess with the deadlines if we aren't careful."

"Smart planning. I love renovations."

"I can tell. Maybe we can walk over there in a little bit so you can see the before, and when we are done, I can show you the after."

Her eyes lit up. "I'd like that," she said. "Why did you say you could tell I liked renovations?"

"The HGTV comment for one, and for two…what's that?"

He nodded in the direction of the nightstand she had been sanding the last few days.

"That's one of my little projects. When I have time, I like to go antique shopping, find pieces that speak to me, and restore it. Most of the time, I add my own modern twist to it. Some pieces I keep, others I sell, and occasionally I donate items to a local women's shelter."

"That's not little at all. It's a big deal—creative and generous. I'm impressed. I do something similar out in California. There is a community for low-income families, and when I have the extra time, my team and I do free repairs and upgrades to the homes."

"Kody," she said, touching her chest, "that is so sweet."

"And so is what you do for the women's shelter," he countered.

"Yeah, helping others is what makes the world go round. It feels good to do something for others. I used to go with my mom when I was a kid to different homeless shelters and serve food. It surely kept me grateful for everything I had. Although I didn't complain much anyway. I had a good life. My time growing up was enjoyable and memorable. I often think back on it, or rewatch some of my favorite shows growing up, to feel closer to it."

"You have a love for throwbacks?"

"I guess you could say that. I feel like the world was safer and somehow saner back then, or maybe it only seemed that way."

"No, I fully understand what you mean. When I watch a movie from the 70s or 80s, with that horrible wallpaper, people rushing to their ringing landline phones and kids coming inside from playing hopscotch all day instead of video games. It really makes you miss it."

She couldn't believe it. He actually understood what she was saying. Not only that, he had a comment of true substance to add to it. Most guys laughed her off or commented that nothing is different or worse, that there are only now just more media outlets to report the bad stuff.

It wasn't that she didn't understand what they were saying or even agree on some level. Social media had definitely opened the floodgates of information, but it still didn't negate the fact that memories of her childhood made her feel better and comforted.

They continued eating their pizza and talking for a couple more hours. After that, they walked next door so that she could see the current state of the property. As he walked her through his plans for the place, she was taken in by the passion and care of the details he put into his work.

She was surprised that she didn't want the night to end. She wasn't sure if she ever enjoyed talking to a guy she'd just met this much.

He told her that he would be over at 9am to get started on the plumbing. He also promised her that the bathroom in her room would be back in full working order no later than Sunday.

In the meantime, since he would start with her bathroom first, she needed to clear her things out so he could get the work done easier. Her bathroom was small, so she didn't have much in there. Also because she had the time, she decided to also clear out the guest bathroom. That way, it would be ready when he wanted to get started.

She glanced at the clock. It was only 9:45. While she was moving around the house, clearing out the bathrooms, she thought that now would be a good time to check in on Chloe and Jessica and catch them up on the events unfolding in her life.

Expectedly Chloe answered the phone, cheerful and ready to chat.

"Are you sure you aren't busy?" Winter asked. "I don't want to interrupt you and Derek."

"Nope. I'm good. Derek is in his office preparing for some upcoming meeting, and I was just painting my toenails. Your timing is perfect. What's up?"

Chloe was mostly quiet the whole time Winter recounted the details of her assault, the plumbing situations and Kody's role in everything. Every now and then, she would gasp and say, "are you kidding?" or laugh where appropriate, but nothing more than that.

When Winter was finally done, Chloe said, "first things first, I'll bet you were scared. I would have pissed myself."

"I think I was too afraid to do much of anything other than try to keep my life intact."

"I am so glad that bastard didn't really get to hurt you. I would have had to hunt him down and kill that piece of shit myself."

"I know. I thank God for Kody being there when he was."

"That brings me to the next thing. This sexy stallion saves you then ends up being one of the guys working next door to you. And you didn't even mention any of this when you came over to shower the other day! If I wasn't so thankful you were ok I'd be so mad with you right now."

"I'm sorry. At first, I didn't want to share the assault when it first happened, then things just started moving too fast. As for Kody, it's crazy, right?! He happens to be living next door while he works on the house."

"Huh? Like he's homeless and some sort of charity case for his job?"

Winter laughed out loud. "Homeless... far from it, I actually think he's loaded. He has a house in California and owns the construction company with his cousin. He moves around between here and his other locations in Texas and California, working on different homes, getting them built, repaired, or whatever they need to get them sold."

"Interesting," she said with an intrigued tone. "I like it. And I think I like this Kody guy for you. Please tell me he is single?"

"He is and I like him, but he's just passing through, and I don't want to jump in line with all the other women I assume are beating down his door."

"Winter, please push those other women over and claim your prize. You said he's single, so you're not being some home wrecker. I'm sure he likes you too, right?"

"I think so. He is offering to do the plumbing work for free."

Chloe was silent for a long moment and then said, "Winter, you must have missed a step. You told me about your plumbing issues, that he gave you an estimate on repairs and that you hired him to do it. Somehow you didn't mention that he was doing it all for free."

"Yeah," Winter said sheepishly, "I skipped that little detail."

"Do I need to come slap you? Of course, he likes you! This man is about to throw away thousands of dollars just to look at your ass, and you are saying you *think* he likes you!"

"It's not completely free; I will at least make him meals once a week."

At that, Chloe started laughing, "for what he is doing, you need to open a restaurant for him and don't forget to add yourself to the menu of available options."

"Only you would have a ton of sex jokes."

"I think anyone in their right mind would. Seriously, though, you know I just talk a lot of crap to mess with you, but it is clear he really likes you. So what if he may leave soon? That's why they have cars, planes and phones. You are basing your reactions on the fact that your past attempts at a long distance didn't work out. Don't do that to yourself."

"I know you're probably right, but I just need to think about it some more. Opening up isn't that easy, time and time again."

"I get that. In the meantime, you will have me pushing you out of the nest, again and again, my little birdie. Don't grow all cold and distant. Yeah, love hurts, but so can being alone if you don't want to be."

It made total sense, but Winter wanted to be careful.

"I hear you, Chloe. I'll try."

"That's all I'm saying."

"I need to call Jessica and check up on her. I'm sure she, too, would like an update on my life."

"Don't bother, she'll be calling you."

"Huh?"

"I was texting her while we were chatting. No way is she going to sit this love story out. The way you two met and now with him living next door, she wants all the details."

Sure enough, Winter heard her phone click, indicating another call coming in.

"And there's Jessica. You want to be added in?"

"Nope, got to go. I'm about to surprise hubby in his office with a happy ending." She giggled mischievously. "Later."

Winter switched over to Jessica, and as soon she said hello, Jessica blurted out, "Oh, Winter, it's just like the movies. Tell me everything!"

For the second time that night, Winter dove into the story of how they met, reconnected, the plumbing drama and how she feels about him. After hearing responses that sounded identical to Chloe's and catching up on what was new in Jessica's life, they ended the call.

She really did love her friends. They were kind, honest, straightforward, hilarious and a whole lot crazy, but she wouldn't have it any other way. A chat with them always made her feel much better and more open to taking risks.

Taking a risk is actually how they all became friends. It was in fourth grade that they bonded over setting up a boy that was bullying them. He was a fifth-grader named Terrell Nash but went by the nickname Terror. He was a lot of trouble and spent most of his time harassing all the other kids in school—making kids cry, stealing their lunch money, or making them fall was all part of his normal day-to-day.

It was Chloe who one day said enough was enough when she found a sad Winter in the corner crying because little terror had snatched off one of her favorite hair bows during recess and wouldn't give it back. Until that point, Chloe hadn't talked much to Winter, but she thought Winter was a nice girl and didn't deserve what Terrell did.

Chloe decided since he liked to steal, maybe she could help him out. So she and Winter made a plan to get him back the next day. Chloe knew where their teacher kept her purse. It was in a closet in the back of the classroom on the top shelf.

The next day, having Winter stand to stand guard, she snuck in and made it to the closet. Using a step stool that was in the corner, she was able to retrieve her teacher's purse. She pulled out her wallet and, for good measure, a pack of gum.

Terror kept his book bag on a table outside during recess, so she planned to slip the items in and later tell a teacher that she saw him do it.

However, on her way out, still holding the wallet and gum in hand, she saw Jessica, who was at the blackboard erasing the lessons from that morning.

Jessica was a straight-A student, labeled teacher's pet, and was always used as an example of how the rest of them should behave. Chloe didn't care for Jessica for those reasons alone, and now Miss goody two-shoes was probably going to rat her out.

To her surprise, Jessica said nothing. Just stared at Chloe wide-eyed. After a moment of just looking at each other, Chloe figured, "what the hell," she'd come this far and tucked the items into her pockets and walked back to the door to go outside.

Successfully planting the evidence in Terror's book bag, she waited until recess was over and then ran up to the teacher, telling her what she saw.

Of course, Terrell denied taking anything. He was outside the whole time he swore to the teacher. Chloe assumed to settle the score, of Chloe's word against his, the teacher might ask the class if anyone else saw Terrell take anything, at which point Winter was supposed to step forward and say she did.

But to Chloe's horror, the teacher didn't do that. Instead, she went inside to ask angelic Jessica if she saw anyone inside the classroom while she was cleaning the board. And of course, Jessica said she did see someone; Chloe rolled her eyes and was ready to surrender when Jessica said she saw Terrell sneaking away with the stolen items. Needless to say, little Terror got in some major trouble, and Winter got new friends.

They had her back then, and they still had it now. They were right, she should stop being so scared. So what if love didn't work out well for her in the past? That didn't mean she should go out of her way to avoid getting to know a great guy.

Maybe if nothing else, he could end up being a good friend that she hung out with when he was in town. He was the type that was impressive on and off paper, and that was a good thing.

With his business mind and easy-going nature, he was definitely a good person to know. It was decided, they could be friends. No one could ever have too many friends, could they?

Even though he was a friend she wanted desperately to sleep with, that didn't have to happen. She could keep it cool and just go with the flow.

Chapter 10
Kody

That was one of the most enjoyable times with a woman Kody had, had in a long time. For the last few years, his dates with women generally consisted of small talk and eventually sex.

But in the past few months, it hadn't consisted of anything because he hadn't had the time or interests to entertain women that he knew he could never be serious with.

The last few dates he went on were with a girl named Keisha, five months before he left California to head to Texas. She lived on the other side of the community he lived in, and they often exchanged pleasantries when he was checking his mail and she was out walking her dog.

She repeatedly hinted at them going out, but he wasn't really sure. She was attractive, had a very nice body and seemed sane enough. Yet somehow, she gave him a weird vibe. However, having nothing concrete to base his internal hesitations on, he finally caved and asked her out to dinner.

In the end, he should have just listened to his instincts. After their second date, it became clear why she wanted to get to know him. She was a divorcee who was only living in the neighborhood because she got the house in the settlement. The problem was she couldn't afford to stay there and keep up with her lavish lifestyle.

It was a comfortable, upscale, gated community, with a 24-hour patrol officer and top of the line amenities. She couldn't keep up with everything with just a basic nine to five.

Therefore, she was hoping to get remarried soon so that someone could keep her living the life she had become accustomed to. She assumed Kody must have made a pretty decent living because he had a home in the neighborhood. She was right about that assumption but wrong that Kody was going to be husband number two.

The magnet effect of money was something that he had become familiar with. Of course, he knew not every woman was out for money, but he had definitely run into his fair share of those who wanted to become Mrs. Benton for all the wrong reasons.

Generally, his looks alone was enough to grab a woman's attention, but when they found out he was pretty well off, they began to press the idea of having a relationship harder.

Usually, he could tell the type from a mile away, and if they did get past his radar, it wasn't long before they revealed themselves in one way or another.

He recalled another woman he was getting to know who was drawn in by how many zeros she assumed were in his bank account. They were at his house watching a movie, and she asked to use the restroom. Pointing her in the direction of it, he continued watching the movie.

After hearing a small noise coming from his home office, he walked towards the sound. She was on the phone with her friend with her back towards the door. He heard her tell the friend that she was looking for his bank statement because she could tell he had money.

He had to give it to her, she was bold. Impressed with her courageous action, he decided to give her another minute to continue her search. She wouldn't find anything, of course.

Anything pertaining to his personal finances was in a safe across the room, hidden by a decorative table. Still casually leaning on the doorframe, he said, "I think you'll have better luck if you look through the papers to your right."

She nearly jumped out of her skin. He still smiles to himself when he thinks about that story.

Yes, he had definitely met his share of women he referred to as "goal minded." Which was why he could tell that Winter was so different. It's as if she called out to him without even saying a word.

Activating his protective mode to want to be there for her, spoil her and do anything to make her smile. He had already broken his own rule of mixing business with pleasure, but he simply could not resist. He wanted to make sure she was taken care of and that the job was done right.

Being a contractor himself, he'd heard the horror stories of crappy work and unprofessional service. He did not want that happening to her.

He was so moved by not only her beauty but her drive, creativity, genuine kindness and strength. She wasn't looking for handouts from him or anyone else. He admired the hell out of that in a woman, and it just made him want her even more.

Money already wasn't a big deal to him; he just wanted to spend it on a woman that he cared for and felt deserved it. And even though he had just met her, he could tell Winter Daniels was one of those women.

The last time he was this taken with a woman was in his mid 20's. Her name was Latisha, but everyone called her Tish, and she was something special. Sadly though, she met the wrong version of Kody. That version was younger and dumber and didn't know a good woman when he saw one.

True, he wasn't looking for a good woman, just more so a good time, but Tish changed all that. She was different. He could tell the first time he met her. The way she carried herself, her goals, her perspective and just overall aura broadcasted her as not typical.

At the time, her mature stance on the world and how she lived in it was a significant contrast to his immature ways and "live life like a party" attitude. At first, he feared getting too close to her.

He understood it to mean that it was the end of easy and careless sex and the beginning of settling down. However, because he genuinely liked her, he tried to be the man he felt she deserved.

They enjoyed each other's company for about a year. They laughed at the same things, finished each other's sentences and could sit quietly for hours, enjoying just being near each other. He had fallen for her, and although he still missed the bachelor life from time to time, he didn't want to let her go.

Then one day, she did what he considered the unthinkable. She invited him to the wedding of her best friend. After that, it was all downhill. His mind switched from rational to irrational faster than ever. He became entirely convinced that she would want to be a bride next.

It was likely his own paranoia, and her invite was innocent. Still, in his adolescent mind, she was basically asking him to plan his own wedding instead of merely attending one. Because he wasn't a total asshole, he didn't leave her hanging. He still accompanied her to the wedding, but afterward, he slowly started to pull away.

He called less, stopped asking her on dates or to come over. She asked him about it a few times, but he just shrugged it off as being busy. Eventually, she stopped pressing the issue and faded away completely. Tish was not the type of woman to keep pleading her case to be a priority to him.

For years thereafter, he thought of her. From his perspective, ending things slowly was letting her down easy. Years down the road, he realized it was the cowards way out, and he had seriously fucked up.

He thought setting her free would, in turn, do the same for him, and he welcomed the idea of returning to his before-Tish lifestyle. The trouble was his body was free, but his heart and mind still seemed to be with her. That's when it became clear to him that not all women were the same and that he liked those that were more of a challenge and lived life with a purpose.

He hadn't gotten that initial feeling he did since Tish, and he assumed he'd never get it again. Accepting that, he focused on the growth of his company, dated women here and there and enjoyed sex with whomever he saw fit.

But now, even the drive for wanting sex with just anyone had disappeared, so he was left with burying himself in work, and for the last few months, that was fine with him. That was until he met Winter.

He knew he felt it the first time he met her, but with their encounter being so brief, he couldn't be absolutely sure. Now, after spending time with her, he was.

In every way that he could, he had to have her. The only drawback was she had walls up. He could see it in her eyes, and it displayed through her cautious actions.

The whole "accidental card throw away" thing didn't fool him. He knew more than likely that was just her way of trying not to get too close. He could see her fighting to not want him, but he knew she did. For now, she saw him as bad news and someone she couldn't trust.

But in time, she would see that she could. He didn't play games, and he would prove it to her; he had no doubt about that.

Sitting at a table that was left in the kitchen area from the work crew a few days ago, he scrolled through his planner. He needed to prep a list of tools he would need and assign timelines for when he would have each step done.

Thinking over the details, he knew he would need a hand with the job.

Already grabbing his phone, he knew who he'd ask. Tim Minter always welcomed overtime. He usually kept his weekends free in case the company had any extra projects. With three kids already and a set of twins on the way, Kody understood Tim's reasoning. He would give Tim a call and let him know which items to bring from the Warehouse.

He could tackle the job himself but getting assistance would help Tim out while ensuring things went smoother. His plan was to give Winter one less thing to stress over before he had to return to California.

Surprisingly, the thought unsettled him. He had just met her, he didn't want to think of leaving her. Surely if feelings did form between them, the distance wouldn't destroy it, would it?

He thought about the long-distance relationship he had with a girl named Ashley, who he met in Georgia the previous year. It didn't work out. However, he reminded himself the circumstances were different, and most importantly, Winter wasn't Ashley.

Deciding to stay away from what may not work, he chose to continue living in the now. For now, she was there, and he would be too.

Getting back to the matter at hand, it was clear the plumbing would be a lot of work, but he wouldn't dare tell her that. He didn't want to give her any reason to shy away from him.

◆◆◆

The next morning, Kody was up bright and early. When the doorbell rang at 8:15, indicating Tim had arrived, they immediately got down to business. Kody explained the timeline and phases he wanted the work completed in. Then he went outside to help Tim unload the truck and carry tools, pipes and drywall over to Winter's yard.

When everything was complete, they walked up the three stairs that led to Winter's front door.

Winter opened the door before Kody even had the chance to knock.

"Well, good morning, beautiful," he said to her.

She was wearing gray and purple drawstring shorts and a white tank top that read, "I'll just sleep it off." Her hair was up in a high ponytail with a few loose pieces that were doing an adorable job of framing her face. He wanted to throw his damn work bag to the side and work on her instead.

She smiled, said good morning, and then invited them in.

Standing in the entryway, Kody put down his work bag and introduced Tim. They shook hands, said their hello and then Kody said, "We are ready to get started."

"I see, and ten minutes early no less. I was making some coffee and saw you guys walking over from the window. Would either of you like a cup?"

"We just had some," Kody said.

"Ok. Well, you know where the bathroom is. Please let me know if you need anything."

Nodding, both men headed to the bathroom, and Winter walked into the living room.

It only took moments before the clanking and banging noises of repairs flooded the house. He was thankful that her house wasn't huge because it meant they would get to the pipes easier and seal things back up faster.

About an hour into working, Kody realized they were missing a part. Going into the living room, he saw Winter sitting at the table typing away on her computer. She looked up at him and smiled.

"Sorry to bother you, would it be ok if we ran to the warehouse to get another part we need? It could wait until tomorrow, but we are working at a good pace, and I don't want to interrupt that. The warehouse is only 15 minutes away, so it won't take long."

"Fine by me."

Kody and Tim were able to quickly retrieve the necessary part from the warehouse because it was Saturday, and no one was there. The only person he would have possibly run into on the weekend was Jackson, and Jackson rarely went into the office since he could do most of his stuff from home.

En route back to Winter's, Kody again went over the plumbing steps in his head to be sure they were using their time effectively. He wanted to be able to at least give her a working shower today. It was looking very possible, but until he got back and made some more adjustments, he couldn't be 100% sure.

He briefly considered leaving Tim to keep working while he was gone. He trusted Tim and had no reason to doubt his professionalism or Winter's safety around him. But he would never do that.

Her attack was still a fresh wound, and being left with a man she had just met wasn't a good call on his end. If he wanted her to open up, he needed to make her always feel protected.

That meant he wouldn't push issues that she wasn't ready to discuss or make any sexual advances right now. That last one was hard because he wanted her so fucking bad, but he knew what she needed was time.

They returned in under an hour and got back to work. At around 1:30, things were looking so good with the plumbing that he was sure he would have her shower ready by the time he was done working for the day. The wall would still be open, but that wouldn't pose a problem to using the shower.

Entering the living room to tell her the good news, he saw her busy moving around in the kitchen. She obviously didn't hear him come in because she didn't look up. He watched her for a moment. He enjoyed seeing her small curvy frame advance around the kitchen as she stepped this way and that, putting food on a white tray. Every time she leaned down, one of her long black curls would fall in her face. He could easily get used to seeing her every day.

Finally, he said, "Winter, do you have a second?"

Picking up the tray, she came around the island and sat what looked to be chicken wraps on the table.

"Sure, what's up?"

"I have good news. We are almost done with the plumbing for your en suite bathroom. We will need to finish up the drywall tomorrow, but you are welcome to use your shower tonight. It's not a pretty sight, but I tried to keep everything as neat as possible so that you would be able to get to your bathroom without too much hassle."

"Thank God!" she said. "When you first walked in, I thought you were going to say you ran into some issues and I would be without my bathroom for another week! But thank you for that, and now I have some good news for you."

He was surprised. Seeing her was good enough for him.

"What is your good news?"

"Lunch is ready."

"Lunch?" he asked.

"Yes, lunch. You didn't think I was going to let you work and not feed you two, did you?"

"Winter, you didn't have to do that; we would have…"

She waved her hand through the air to cut his response.

"It is no trouble, and it provides the perfect segue into what else I wanted to ask you. What do you think about dinners Saturday and Sunday? It just seems weird having you work here and then go order takeout at home alone."

"I think your new offer sounds great."

"Wonderful. Now you can have lunch whenever you're ready, and if seven works for you tonight, I will see you for dinner."

He agreed, and they all sat down for lunch.

♦♦♦

That evening, he was on time, as usual. Winter had just started setting the table when he arrived. He offered to give her a hand, but she declined, saying most of the work was already done. She told him to make himself comfortable, and he did so by looking around the small but cozy living room.

On one side of the fireplace, she had built-in bookshelves. She displayed various objects such as books, tiny decor pieces and artwork. Neatly in the corner of the bottom shelf were several board games. Kody leaned in to take a closer look.

"I see you have trouble and monopoly. Those are two of my favorite games."

"They may be your favorite, but I, Mr. Benton, am the champ."

"I'd like to see you prove that," he said.

"Careful what you wish for," she responded.

Coming around the kitchen island, she placed two plates on the table. "Dinner is ready."

They dined on perfectly seasoned steaks, paired with mashed potatoes and a spinach salad. The food was delicious, and he wasn't even the slightest bit surprised that she was a good cook.

They talked all through dinner about any and everything, and before they knew it, they had finished their meal and moved over to the couch to get comfortable.

"What were you like in high school?" he asked.

"Oh, wow. It seems like it was so long ago. But to answer your question, I was a mess, completely consumed with all the teenage girl drama—I'm too fat. I want to be popular. I'm in love with this guy. Then next week, it's that guy. You know, the crazy hormonal "I know it all" ride that most teenagers are on? Well, it didn't skip over me. I was right there in it, moody and thinking my world was over, every time the slightest negative thing happened. My good friends, Chloe, Jessica and I were cheerleaders, and that was fun. But overall, I would never want to live through those years again."

"I remember you telling me about your friends. They sound nice. Chloe is the one that just got married, right?"

"Yes, and Jessica is the event planner who planned it."

He nodded, then said, "Do you ever want to get married?"

She was caught off guard by his question. "I do. But who knows, relationships can be so tricky."

"True," he said, agreeing with her.

"What about you?"

"I'd love to be married one day," he said.

She was surprised because she kind of expected him to give some non-committal answer to the question.

"Wait," she said, nudging his leg. "You didn't even tell me about how you were in high school. Let me guess, you were a jock and a real ladies' man."

"Sadly, that does describe me. I spent way too much time enjoying the glory of being the it guy and a lot less time understanding that being "it" could do nothing for me. I didn't apply myself as much as I should have and got in trouble a lot."

"No judgments here; none of us were our best selves in high school. Any high school sweethearts?"

"No, as you said, I was a ladies' man, so I really wasn't interested in dating just one girl."

She nodded as if his immature ways in high school were still alive and well, in the man he was today.

She then confirmed his suspicions when she said, "Yeah, that doesn't surprise me."

"I'd never deny the truth," he said. "That was me from high school and basically until my mid 20's".

"Ok. So why should I believe it's not you now?"

"Something you should know about me, I don't beat around the bush. If I ask it, I want to know it. If I say it, it's because I mean it, and if I think it, it's usually because I'm going to do it."

Winter shifted as if the temperature in the room must have gone up a few notches, which meant she understood Kody perfectly. If he wanted it, he got it, and what he wanted was her.

"Now you are about more than sex and games, but that use to be all you were about."

"Bingo," he said.

"If you say so."

"I do say so. And don't try to avoid the topic. Did you have a high school sweetheart?"

"No. I dated a few different guys but nothing serious."

"Interesting," he said.

"How so?"

"Well, just like I seem like such a bad boy to you. You strike me as a good girl. One that is very old-fashioned in her way of doing things."

"I guess in ways I am. I mean, I wasn't like you, just having sex with everyone. I actually stayed a virgin all throughout high school."

He noticed she quickly averted his eyes as if she said something or gave some insight into herself that she didn't mean to.

Smiling, he said, "I guess you are as much a good girl as you seem."

"Whatever," she responded, playfully rolling her eyes.

"No, seriously, I think that's cool."

Somehow, that made her even sexier to him. He wished, at that moment, he could kiss her, yank her down to the floor and have his way with her. But he knew he couldn't, now was not the time.

"You said earlier you enjoyed board games. Want to play a few rounds of trouble?" she asked.

He thought that was a good idea because the game title was fitting for precisely what she'd be in if she kept sitting this close to him, for much longer.

Chapter 11
Winter

The next day was more of the same—loud noise as Kody and Tim worked on the house. She was grateful that she had been able to take a shower last night. True to his word, they only left a small amount of mess that she was able to maneuver around quite quickly and easily.

Preparing lunch for them again, she was sure that she had to do something special for him. He had only requested dinners on Sunday. She had decided to toss in lunch on both days and add dinners on Saturday, but it still didn't feel like enough.

Maybe she could give him a nice thank you gift. She liked the idea, but she didn't have a clue as to what to get him.

At dinner that night, they enjoyed Chicken Curry with garbanzo beans, onions and peppers, over a bed of jasmine rice. She decided to pair the meal with a glass of wine. Even though she'd seen him in regular clothes, she still half expected to see him in his white tank top and work jeans when she opened the door.

But like last night, he was dressed casually in jeans and a white and dark blue shirt. The observation made her ask him how he handled laundry during renovations, for which he informed her that he always kept four weeks' worth of clothes with him during a renovation. The wardrobe consisted of work clothes, casual clothes and a couple of suits for business meetings.

Although the home had a washer and dryer, he took his worn clothes to the cleaners every two weeks, and it helped him stay in proper rotation.

She asked him more about his company and how it all got started to keep him talking because she loved hearing his voice and staring at his lips. She knew, without a doubt, they had to be soft, and he was probably an amazing kisser.

When the night was over, she gave him a hug. Mentally, she blamed it on the alcohol, but there was no need because her invitation for increased contact was well received. Kody held her close and gently caressed the small of her back.

His hard body framed against hers almost made her abandon her will power and yank him down for a kiss. But right before she threw caution and her panties to the wind, Kody leaned down, kissed her on the cheek and said goodnight.

◆◆◆

The next morning before work, she decided to send him a quick text. She had just showered in her completely repaired and freshly painted bathroom and had to say thank you.

She texted: *"Hi Kody. Thanks again for the repairs. Now every time I shower, I'll think of you."*

"Should I say that? Aren't I supposed to be keeping my distance? It is just so hard. Technically, I would think of him because he fixed it. That was innocent enough, right? Would he read too much into that? Do I want him to?"

Hitting send before she could talk herself out of it, she tossed her phone in her purse and finished getting ready.

The workday was slow. They were wrapping up two projects and hadn't begun work on the new ones.

At around 12, Lisa popped her head in. "Hey, Winter, you got a minute?"

"Sure, what's up"?

Lisa came in and sat down. Then leaned back and closed her eyes.

"Um, are you ok?"

"Yeah, I'm fine, just hiding from Mr. Sanders."

"Why?"

"I had ten minutes left on my break. He found me sitting at my desk and started this long conversation about how he had the perfect guy for me. I was a little intrigued at first, and then I found out he was talking about his nephew, Dylan."

She made a face to match the obvious disgust she had on the inside, and reflexively, Winter did the same.

Dylan was Mr. Sanders forty-something year old nephew who was always trying to hook up with someone. The task seemed simple enough, but it was a challenge because Dylan was gross.

He was immature, dressed sloppy and had no ambition. He was living in Mr. Sanders's basement for what must have now been four years. From time to time, he'd show up at the studio attempting to flaunt his relation to Mr. Sanders as a way to get dates.

He flirted with every girl there and tossed around outdated pickup lines to, as he called it, "seal the deal." Winter once had the unfortunate experience of being subjected to his company for an entire hour.

She didn't want to be rude, so she tried her hardest to wait him out in hopes that he would see a short skirt walk by that he couldn't bear to ignore.

However, after she made a comment about being sleepy and he said, "girl, you must be tired cause you been running through my mind all day," her patience vanished. She put her phone to her ear, faked answering an emergency call, and excused herself to her office, where she hid out the rest of the day.

Not too heartbroken by her absence, she heard through work gossip that he moved on to one of the director's assistants.

"Enough said," she stated to Lisa. "Hide away."

Turning her attention back her computer, she realized she hadn't checked her phone since she got to work. When she glanced at the screen, she immediately began smiling to herself. Her alerts indicated she had a text message from Kody. She clicked on it in anticipation.

It read: *"You are very welcome. I'm glad to hear you'll think of me in the shower; my skills are the reason you are wet after all."*

She bit her lip and grinned to herself. She wasn't going to reply to that. If she did, he was likely to have her getting wet right there in her office, no shower required. Wasn't she supposed to be keeping it casual? There was only a friendship in their future, nothing more.

But the idea of sex with him managed to turn her on and scare her. Which was odd. It's not like she was scared of sex.

Maybe it was just that her attraction to him was unlike any she'd ever had. Liking a guy this much and this fast was brand new for her. She wanted him, and every day she felt her desires would override her reasonings.

"What has you smiling like that?" Lisa said, staring at Winter suspiciously.

"Oh, nothing."

"Yeah, right, either it's a man or the test said negative."

"You are so silly. I'll give you a hint; it isn't a test."

"Good, it's a man. Do we like him?" Lisa asked excitedly.

"We do, but we're just friends."

"Boo," Lisa said.

"I need to hear about some real love. Staging all these scenes are really messing with my mind. I need to either experience my own fairytale or live vicariously through someone else's romantic reality."

"Sorry to disappoint."

"No biggie. I've got work to do anyway. I think I have successfully dodged Mr. Sanders, so I'm going to help them bring in some equipment from outside."

"Why, are they about to start another scene? I didn't see any more on the schedule."

"No. It looks like it's about to rain, so they want to move some things in."

"Oh, wow. Then they'll have to move it right back out for tomorrow, huh?"

"Not likely. I checked the forecast. I think it's going to rain all week."

"Damn. Sucks for their budget."

"Yes, it does. Later."

She waved goodbye to Lisa.

If they couldn't do the outdoor scenes for the rest of the week, that would create a pile-up of work for next week, which wasn't good because next week was already full.

But that was a problem for next week, no need to borrow stress. Instead, she could use this downtime to locate an acceptable gift for Mr. Sanders's niece. She still had no idea what to get.

It did indeed rain for the rest of the week. But anything that pushed the intense heat of August out for some cooler weather was worth the gloomy, gray water-filled days. Besides, she had other things to lift her spirits. She and Kody had been texting and chatting on the phone all week.

He made her laugh, and hearing his voice made her feel alive in indescribable ways. Even though he lived next door, she rarely saw him because the rainy days kept him and his team mostly indoors doing repairs. If he wasn't working inside the home, he was at his warehouse, tending to other business.

Arriving home Thursday, she was glad there was only one more workday left in the week. She was ready to see Kody again and knew from his message a half hour ago, he felt the same. It appeared she was throwing her own advice about not getting too close to him right out the window.

Then again, they hadn't done anything more than talk and enjoy one another's company, so maybe there was still hope for her. It was nice being his friend, and besides the flirtatious comment about the shower making her think of him, there hadn't been any more naughty notes delivered.

Opening the fridge and then closing it almost immediately after, she concluded she didn't have much of an appetite. With work being so slow all week, she spent most of her days sitting at her desk and snacking like crazy.

Walking over to the nightstand that was now ready for a fresh coat of paint, she decided to work on it for a few hours and then get ready for bed. She turned on the TV, and instantly, HGTV came roaring to life. She needed it for inspiration and background noise while she worked.

As the time ticked by, Winter half-listened to the episodes as they played out. Every now and again, she would take a brief pause to see the house before the remodel and then again once it was complete.

As a new episode was starting up, she took her anticipated break. This couple wanted a home with a long list of features, including at least four baths, five bedrooms, a large kitchen, an office area, a deck, a pool and a large space for entertaining.

As the show host took them around to see homes that had the potential to meet the couple's many requests, she was caught off guard when they showed one of the homes.

It had nearly fifteen bolts on the door. The husband on TV made some comment that the previous owners must have been obsessed with security.

Winter glanced at her own door. Just the one lock stared back at her. After her whole ordeal, she should have considered making sure she was a lot safer in her own home.

May as well add figuring out how to better secure the premises to the growing list of ways to protect herself. She already had to find a way to stop those awful sporadic nightmares and learn to defend herself on there.

She truly had her work cut out for her, and sadly, she didn't want to face any of it.

◆◆◆

She woke with a jerk. The man with the knife had her.

She shoved at her covers and realized… No, he didn't. It was just a dream. A fucking dream. No one had her. She was safe in her bed at home. She took a few deep breaths and looked at her clock. It was 11:30.

She was safe; she was fine. If only her heart would get back into her chest, she would be able to collect herself. It was only a dream.

But it felt so real—his breath on the back of her neck and the cold, sharp blade at the front. He held it with just enough pressure to slice her clean open if she made the wrong move.

"Not real. Not real," she said aloud.

Then she heard it, a sound at her window. Getting out of bed hesitantly, she tiptoed over to the window. Gathering her nerves, she risked a tiny peek out into the rainy dark night.

She saw nothing. More so importantly, she saw no one. Maybe it was just a loose branch or thunder in the distance. She did hear there was a major thunderstorm rolling in. She got back in bed, did three rounds of slow, steady inhales and exhales, then closed her eyes.

As she slowly drifted back to sleep, she saw it again… the knife! At the same time, a powerful bolt of lightning cracked the sky. Shaking and beyond terrified, she grabbed her pillow, and suddenly the room went absolutely dark.

"No no no no no," she said, reaching towards her nightstand and pulling out a large flashlight.

"Did someone cut my power? Is someone trying to break in? Did sitting in bed like an idiot give them ample time to do so? I need a weapon. How in the hell do I not have a weapon? All I have is a stupid flashlight! What would I do with that? Hope the light catches his eye just right and momentarily blinds him so I can get away? This is ridiculous. He'd stab me to death while laughing at me."

"Calm down, Winter," she said aloud. Hearing her own voice offered no reassurance as it sounded shakier than she expected.

First things first, she would check the window again. Maybe the power went out through the whole neighborhood. If that wasn't the case, she would make her way to the kitchen and grab a knife. Maybe she should consider switching the order of things and getting the knife before checking the window, but the window was right there.

What if someone really was trying to break in? She might get lucky this time and another quick glance out the window would provide her with a glimpse of them. Then, she could dial 911 while running to the kitchen to grab the sharpest knife in the drawer.

Holding her cellphone in one hand and the flashlight in the other, she peeked once again out the window. She released a huge breath when she saw darkness throughout the neighborhood.

No one had singled her out; the power was out through the entire community. She was finally getting her nerves to accept that there was likely no threat when her cellphone began to vibrate in her hand. The sudden movement caused her to drop the heavy flashlight, and she let out a curse as it landed on her foot.

Picking up the phone, she saw an indication for a text. It was from Kody.

It read: *"Are you ok?"*

"No," she texted back before she even thought about it.

She sat there for about thirty seconds, trying to decide if her response to him made her sound weak. Ultimately, she didn't care. This was no time to play strong. She was scared, and even sleep offered no escape. Mistake or not, she couldn't take it back now.

She heard a knock on the door and Kody's voice calling her name.

Grabbing the flashlight, she rushed to open it.

Coming inside, he touched her shoulder and then her face. With concern etched on his face, he said, "What's wrong? Are you alright?"

She could only nod. Had this man literally just run over, no questions asked to save her… again?

"What happened?" he asked, looking around the dark room.

She had the flashlight facing the wall behind him. The positioning offered enough light so that they could make out each other and their immediate surroundings, but nothing more.

Choosing her words carefully, she said, "The thunder must have woken me up. Then with the power going out shortly after and sounds of what I think must have been branches hitting my window, I guess I just got scared."

She wouldn't tell him about the nightmare. She already felt pathetic enough. She had spent many nights alone in this house without power. It was embarrassing that just because she had been attacked, things that were once so normal were now so scary.

Looking up at him, she asked, "Did you literally drop everything and rush over here?"

"Yeah," he said. "I was up working when I heard the thunder. After the power went out, I thought of you, so I decided to text to make sure you were good. I figured if you didn't respond, you were likely asleep. When you did and said you weren't ok, I rushed right over. I don't even think I shut the front door."

She didn't know what to say. No man had ever seemed to care about her this much.

"Listen. I'm going to go next door and get a couple of things and lock up the house. I will be back in less than 2 minutes. Will you be ok?"

"Of course, I will," she said.

He exited the house, and she turned around, shining the light throughout her living room. There was nothing out of place, and no vengeful man with a knife had been lurking in the darkness. But seeing she had nothing to fear still didn't settle her unease. Hearing the thunder crackle and pop in the distance, she prayed he would get back quick.

Her prayers were answered when he walked back into her house less than a minute later, carrying some big bulky object. He placed it in the living room and pressed a button. Instantly the whole area lit up.

"Wow. It's kinda like the lights are back on," she said.

The light was so bright, her flashlight became nothing more than a glow stick in comparison. She switched it off and was once again thankful that her house wasn't that big. By placing the light in the living room, the entryway and kitchen area were now also illuminated.

"The power just went out a few minutes ago; I'm surprised you already had something like this," she said.

"I keep it on the truck. It's useful for when I'm working late or on a site that doesn't have power yet."

"Thank God for your smart planning," she said.

They moved to the couch and sat down.

"Cute pajamas," he said.

"Thanks," she said, looking down. She was wearing an all-red set, with white letters that read "Nap time is my happy hour."

"What were you working on?" she asked.

"Computer work from a few of our past projects."

"I hope the power outage didn't cause you to lose something you can't get back."

"No, everything is fine. I'm always prepared. Tell me what made you say you weren't ok on the text again."

"I already told you, it was the thunderstorm. I think everything caught me off guard. Why are you asking again?"

He touched her hand and said in a tone that somehow indicated he knew she wasn't being completely honest, "because I feel a person should have to look you in the eyes when they are being dishonest with you."

She exhaled audibly. "Ok, you got me. I had another nightmare."

"Why didn't you call me? I told you, you can always call me."

"Yeah, but people just say that. They don't really mean it. It's just a common line that people use. Usually to fill the silence."

"Winter, I told you. If I say it, I mean it."

He pulled her into his arms. She laid on his chest, and he kissed her forehead. Overwhelmed with his kindness and care on a matter so delicate and scary for her gave her the push she needed to open up and talk to him about her reoccurring nightmares.

She fell asleep in his arms and slept soundly until the beeping sounds of appliances and random devices sprung back to life, indicating the power was on.

Chapter 12
Winter

The next few weeks went by fast. It was Sunday, and Winter was preparing for the last originally arranged dinner for the work Kody was completing. She wasn't too broken up about it because they had already decided to continue hanging out.

Neither of them wanted their time together to end. So even though they were already having dinners Saturdays and Sundays, as of last week, they also spent time with each other during the week and talked on the phone or texted every day.

He not only had taken care of all the plumbing, but he had been there as a shoulder for her to lean on. Her nightmares had reared its horrific head several times over the last few weeks, and every time she needed him, he came without question.

He'd stay as long as she needed him to and kept her mind occupied by playing board games, watching movies or just talking.

He never pushed for sex, and she liked that; in some twisted way, it made her want him more. But the pain of how hurt she would be if things didn't work out kept her in line... mostly. She still cuddled close to him and enjoyed the gentle kisses on her forehead and cheek he'd often give her. But shockingly, she still hadn't kissed him. However, she could tell that it was a fight she was about to lose very soon—might be tonight, even.

Turning off the water in the kitchen sink, she marveled at how great things looked. Everything worked perfectly and you couldn't tell where the new drywalling and paint started and where the untouched parts ended.

Kody and Tim finished up around 11a.m. that morning. Kody said he needed to shower and take care of a few work things before joining her at 7 for dinner.

It was now 6:50, and she was making the sauce for some homemade hot wings. She decided to make today's dinner a bit more fitting to the mood. With it being the end of September, football season had started, and they were excited to watch the game.

Winter loved football. She was dressed in her Atlanta Falcons jersey and a cute fitted pair of black shorts. Pouring the sauce over the wings and adding them to a platter, she was ready to cheer on the Falcons and enjoy some time with Kody.

The doorbell rang, and she went to let him in.

"Smells good. Need me to do anything?" he said, joining her in the kitchen.

"Nope, I got it. Go sit down. I'll bring the wings and beers to the table."

She got them all set up, then turned up the volume on the TV. When they were done eating, they did what they always did and moved their cheering and shouting over to the couch.

During a commercial break, Kody said, "I need to ask you something?"

"What's up?"

"Would you like to go out to a company function with me? One of the investors we work with hosts an annual party that Jackson and I attend. It's next Saturday, and I would be honored if you were my date."

"I'd love to. What time?"

"I can pick you up at seven?"

"Pick me up? I can just walk next door, and we go from there."

"You could, but you won't because it is a date, and *I* —" he said with emphasis on the word, "—am going to pick you up."

She did love his gentleman qualities.

"Excuse me then, your way sounds great. I'm surprised you're asking me out on a date. I just assumed you preferred not being seen with me in public," she said jokingly.

"That couldn't be further from the truth. You are gorgeous, and I think you know that."

He picked up his beer to take another sip.

"Thank you. And you, Kody Benton, are also very handsome," she said, giving him a flirtatious smile.

Placing his beer back on the coffee table coaster, he sat back on the couch and said, "Well, well, what do we have here? I think that is the first time you have verbally admitted your attraction to me."

She frowned. "Really?" she said. "Surely, I have told you."

"Nope."

"What about when…"

"Nope."

"There was that time," she attempted yet again, words fading on her lips as she couldn't recall an example.

"No. You smile, you avert your eyes, you even sigh in that way you do when you really want something, but you feel you shouldn't have it. But you never say it. Don't worry, though, Winter, I already know you want me."

"Do you?" She said, crossing her arms. "How?"

He watched her for a moment, causing her to shift uncomfortably to avoid his sexy, poker-faced gaze. Then he said, "Come here."

Winter moved closer to him. Placing his hand on her exposed thigh, he gently traced one finger up her soft, chocolate-covered skin. Then he moved closer, wrapped his arm around her waist and lifted her onto his lap.

Stopping mere inches from her lips, he said, "because I want you just as bad." Then their lips met.

Soft and teasingly at first and then more intense and passionate. Her mind was exploding. He was a magnificent kisser. She felt tingles all over her body, and the yearning in between her thighs was growing stronger with every second his mouth was on hers. She didn't want to stop, didn't want to pull away. She could stay like this forever.

"That was nice," she said when they finally had to take a breath.

"It was," he agreed.

"Why is it you've never tried to kiss me before?"

"Because you weren't ready."

He was right. If he tried too soon, she may have kissed him but would likely have regretted it almost instantly. She promised herself over a year ago that she would start taking her time, and tonight she felt she had done that. Kissing him felt right, and she found peace in that.

"Thankfully, I am now," she said and leaned in to kiss him again.

◆◆◆

The following Friday, she couldn't stop smiling. Bringing a long and productive work week to an end and getting ready for her first date with Kody the next night had her feeling exhilarated.

Holding the phone to her ear and standing in front of her closet, with dresses strewn about the room, she was starting to feel anxious.

"What type of dress should I wear to this event?"

"That's easy," Chloe said. "One that says fuck me."

"Clo."

"Fast."

"Clo."

"And hard."

"CHLOE!"

Chloe laughed and then said, "Fine! Since you are such a prude, let me think about it."

After a few seconds of silence, she said, "I got it! Wear that glamorous teal number that you wore to the Gibson's charity event. Kody will have to use all of his restraint not to attack you on the dance floor."

Winter imagined it. Chloe was right; it would be perfect. The dress had a v cut around the chest area; it hugged her curves while simultaneously achieving a flowy effect. It was the ideal combination of sexy and classy and was sure to make a good impression. The look on Kody's face when she stepped out in that beauty would keep his eyes locked on her all night.

"I agree," Winter said into the receiver. "I also think wearing my hair up will add a nice touch."

"Doesn't matter; once the night is over, he's going to ruin that hair."

Laughing, Winter said, "Does your mind ever leave the gutter?"

"Not really. I think I've started getting mail there. Anyway, as usual, I have to go, tons of work to do."

"Alright, Clo. Thanks so much."

"Anytime, sweetie. Love you."

"Love you too," Winter said, ending the call.

◆◆◆

The next night, Kody arrived on her doorstep looking every bit of the striking gentleman that he was. He wore a dark blue suit that she could tell from its style and tailored fit, that it carried a hefty price tag. As he walked her down the stairs and toward the vehicle, he held her hand.

Once at the luxurious, black SUV, he opened the door for her and helped her in. She loved how he put one hand on her waist and the other on her ass as he gently guided her into the car. Walking around to his side, he got in, buckled up and they were off.

The buttery leather seat was warm and inviting. Looking around at the wood details, speakers that read "Bose," and the impressive system sitting in front of her, she assumed the vehicle must have been what they called "fully loaded." She had no idea you could rent vehicles that looked like this.

"Nice vehicle. Where did you rent it, if you don't mind me asking?"

"I didn't. It's mine. I leave a vehicle at my Georgia and Texas location for when I'm in town. I only use it when I have meetings or don't want to drive the work van around. Sometimes I let the onsite managers use it so that it doesn't sit around for months without being driven."

"That's smart," she said. She truly didn't know what else to say. He was obviously financially well off, and she didn't want to ask more questions or seem like she was prying. So instead, she leaned back, place her hand over his and enjoyed the rest of the ride listening to the old school R&B station he had playing on the radio.

Arriving at the event, Winter felt glamorous. Not just because Kody had already told her so many times, but the place where the event was being held was nothing short of incredible. It reminded her of one of those red carpet events you see on TV.

Leading Winter over to a man and woman that looked to be about their age, Kody introduced her to his cousin Jackson and Jackson's wife, Erica.

"We finally get to meet the woman Kody is always talking about," Jackson said.

Surprised at being informed that Kody had mentioned her, often it seemed, to one of the closest people in his life, really touched her. She said hello and then shook Jackson's and Erica's hand.

You could tell Kody and Jackson were related. Although Jackson carried more weight in the midsection, they both sported those tall, muscular frames and possessed the type of handsome look that would make most women look twice.

Erica was tall and exotic looking. She had a light brown complexion, dark brown, slanted eyes and high cheekbones. Her hair was cut into a sleek, black, shoulder-length bob that made her look that much fancier.

They all continued chatting for another thirty minutes or so, and then promising to return shortly, Kody pulled Winter away to the dance floor.

"Your cousin and his wife are really nice and funny," she said.

"Yeah, they are really good people."

"I'm surprised you mentioned me to them."

"Why is that?" He asked, leading her slowly to the music with his hand around her waist.

"I don't know, honestly."

"You shouldn't be. Even though I haven't known you long, you're special to me."

She was touched by his words and didn't want to hide that she felt the same. Looking up at him, she said, "You're special to me too, Kody.

A slow smile crossed his lips.

"How tall are you?" she asked.

"6"2", why?"

"I was just curious."

"Don't worry, the far distance from your lips to mine won't make me kiss you any less."

Winter laughed.

"You are so charming and handsome." Then teasingly, she added, "but your belief that I want a kiss from you is a little presumptuous if you ask me."

"Lucky me, I wasn't asking," he said, leaning down to kiss her.

It was soft and sweet and made her weak at the knees.

When the song was over, he led her out onto the balcony, where the view literally took her breath away. She had never seen downtown Atlanta from an angle like this with its dramatic skyline and overflow of tall and short nicely lit buildings. She could stare at it for hours. Kody put his arms around her, and they silently watched the busy city before them.

"Don't you have more people you need to mingle with?"

Not really. I spotted the host when I came in. He was already engaged in what looked to be an intense conversation with a group of people," so I will circle back around to him in a bit. Besides him, I only know another handful of people here."

"As long as I'm not keeping you from anything?"

He wrapped his arms tighter around her waist and kissed her neck. "You aren't."

Then not too far behind him, he heard Jackson calling his name.

"But I'll bet that's about to change if Jackson has anything to say about it."

Jackson approached Kody and Winter with a big grin on his face and said, "Winter, do you mind if I steal Kody away for a second? I have someone I need him to meet."

"Not at all," she said.

Kody gave her one last quick kiss on the lips, and then he and Jackson walked away.

She once again faced the city lights and continued to admire the stunning view laid out before her. This was nice, having a lovely night out with Kody and getting to see parts of his world. It made her feel more connected to him. She really could get used to this.

"Beautiful, isn't it?"

She turned to see a beautiful woman. She was wearing an absolutely breathtaking black dress that hugged her perfect figure and somehow made Winter feel underdressed.

"Yes, it is," Winter said.

The woman offered Winter a small dainty hand. "Seems we haven't had the chance to meet; I'm Ashley."

Shaking her hand, Winter said, "nice to meet you, Ashley. I'm Win—"

"Winter Daniels, I know."

Caught off guard, Winter said, "How?"

"I handle the guest list for the Gander Company events. It's kind of my job to know who is hanging around these things, you know?"

With a relieved smile, Winter said, "Oh, ok, makes sense."

"I see you're here with Kody Benton. Not to be too forward, but from one girl to another, I just wanted to warn you."

"About…" Winter said with alarm bells prematurely sounding in her head.

"He's a liar, or possibly a player, whatever fits for the month, I guess."

"I'm not sure what you're…"

"I know," Ashley said, holding up one perfectly manicured hand. "It's none of my business, but from what I can see, you seem into him. I was once right where you are. I met him at this exact party a year ago, in fact. I really thought the relationship was going somewhere. Long story short, I was wrong and ended up broken-hearted. I just don't want what happened to me to happen to you. Kody isn't the settling down type. So my advice to you is to have your fun, but don't let your heart get involved."

Winter nodded slowly, "um, thanks."

"It's no problem. Us girls have to stick together. Thankfully, even though he might be a waste of time, at least he's a beast in the bedroom, right?"

Ashley said, laughing as if she didn't have a care in the world.

Winter wanted to punch her.

"Right," Winter said, pretending to know anything at all about what sex with Kody was like.

"I have to get back. It was nice meeting you, Winter."

"Likewise," Winter said.

Then as if she hadn't just totally destroyed Winter's world, she turned around after taking a few steps and cheerfully said, "by the way, cute dress." Then, she was gone, leaving Winter stunned.

◆◆◆

Winter just sat there on the ride home, letting the questions, fears, and love scenes between Ashley and Kody consume her. Running into Ashley had thrown her into a loop she didn't see coming. Kody appeared so genuine in his intentions toward her, but then again, didn't every guy?

"Dammit, why now?" she thought.

They were having a wonderful evening, and then here comes Little Miss Ashley, raining all levels of drama on her parade. She didn't want to just believe Ashley, but she didn't want to totally disregard her either. If her past had taught her anything, it was to pay attention to all the signs.

She liked Kody, more than liked—he was the type she could truly love. Her heart told her that he was honest and worth the risk, but her heart was known to confuse what it wanted with what it needed.

Breaking the silence, she said, "Can I ask you a question?"

"Sure," Kody said.

"What's the real reason you did the work for me?"

"You mean besides the obvious?"

"Yes. I know the work needed to be done, but why for free?"

"But it wasn't free, remember those delicious meals," he said.

"Kody. I'm serious. Why?"

"You're a smart girl, Winter. I don't think I need to tell you that I liked you from the first day I met you."

"I understand that. But you could have simply asked me out on a date, couldn't you?"

"I could have, and if necessary, I would have. But at the time, I had an in, and I took it."

"So it wasn't a ploy to get me to owe you something in return, something like sex?"

He said nothing for a long moment and then, "Winter, with all due respect, I don't have to give out free labor to get a woman to sleep with me."

"Don't remind me," she said, rolling her eyes.

"Is something wrong?" he asked, replacing his lighthearted tone with a concerned one.

This conversation was going all wrong really fast. They'd had a magnificent night; she didn't want to ruin it. She just needed to know the truth. What did he want from her?

Deciding to just go ahead and come out with it, she said, "I met Ashley, and she had some interesting things to say about you."

"Ahhh," he said with understanding dawning on him. "I'll bet she did."

"Why do you say that?"

Kody took a deep breath and then exhaled. "I met Ashley last year when I came here for the annual Gander company event. Long story short, we ended up dating long distance for a few months. From the start, I told her I didn't want anything serious, and even though she agreed, when it came down to it, she wanted more than I was looking for. When I broke it off with her, she was pretty mad. Claimed I lied to her and lead her on."

"Did you?"

"I just told you I didn't."

"Why didn't you want to be serious with her?"

"She just isn't my type."

"Why not?"

Kody exhaled again.

"Why do you keep doing that?" Winter asked.

"Doing what?"

"Exhaling before you answer me. Are my questions annoying you?"

Was she trying to pick a fight? Wanting to halt this amazing night in its tracks because she was starting to get scared again? Or was she jealous that, however short-lived, he'd had something with Ashley? No matter the answer, if Ashley was right, her fears of getting hurt were just around the corner.

Still carrying the same calm tone he always did, he said, "No, Winter, you aren't annoying me."

"What is it then?"

"I have the feeling that Ashley got into your head. I like you a lot, and I don't want you to see me in an unfavorable light for untrue reasons. I didn't want more, but she did. That's pretty much the whole story. But you are welcome to ask me anything you like, and I'll always answer honestly."

Winter didn't know what to think. He could be telling her what she wanted to hear. Or Ashley could truly be a nut job, spreading untruths about Kody due to hurt feelings. Winter decided to err on the side of caution. If she didn't sleep with him, she didn't have to worry about getting hurt. They could hang out, still kiss but nothing more. She could keep it light around him... she had to.

Then again, who was she kidding? She was already in too deep with him. She was extremely attracted to him and wanted him so bad it almost physically hurt. Feeling frustrated, she turned to stare out the window.

"You ok?" She heard him say.

Aware that she was letting her emotions show way more than she should for a man she wasn't even in a relationship with, she nodded. Then realizing that he probably didn't see her, she added, "I'm just tired. I had a really nice night. I haven't done dinner and dancing in a long time. Thanks for inviting me."

He placed his hand on hers. "It was my pleasure."

She felt her pulse rise.

"Just stay cool," she mentally told herself. "Stop envisioning him pulling this truck over, laying you on this hood, and…"

She had to stop. She wasn't some horny teenager. So what if Ashley referred to his sex skills as if they ranked off the charts or that he looked extra sexy tonight and harbored a dangerously captivating touch. She could… no, she *would* keep it casual and light. No sex.

"Since we are being honest," he said. "Why don't you tell me why I make you nervous."

"You don't make me nervous," Winter lied.

"Ok," Kody said.

As usual, he wasn't going to push; he never did when it came to delicate matters. That was one more thing she liked about him.

"It's just," she paused. "You seem like this total package. Not only are you handsome and successful, but you are also kind and a gentleman.

Then you top it all off with these ways of looking at people that I'm sure makes women fall apart."

As they drove, the lights from other cars and street fixtures momentarily illuminated the inside of the car. He glanced at her and gave her a smile that had to be saying something; she just wasn't sure what.

"See like that," she said.

"Like what?"

"That little smile you're doing, what were you just thinking?"

"Kody licked his lips and then looked over at her. Do you really want to know what I'm thinking?"

She faced the road. "On second thought, let's just change the subject."

"If you'd like," he said.

"Why wasn't Ashley your type?"

"I think we had conflicting views on the way we saw the world. Not to mention, she came from a lot of money, and it seemed she looked down on people who didn't."

Not even knowing Ashley, Winter could see how that statement would ring true. The "cute dress" comment seemed more condescending than anything.

"Care to give an example?" she asked.

"One time, we were taking a walk and saw this homeless guy. He asked for money for food, and I stopped to give it to him. I only had $50 on me at the time, so I gave him that. After we walked away, she started in on how that was way too much money to give a guy who more than likely only wanted it for drugs. When I told her that could be the case, or he could really just be down on his luck, she said that he's down on his luck because he was lazy. I'm not really one to argue when I see a person has their mind set on something, so I just told her I understood her point and tried to move on. But she couldn't let it go and even went as far as saying I should go back and check to see if the guy did, in fact, buy food. Needless to say, I ended the night early. We hung out for a few more weeks after that, but she was still always making comments that reflected poor opinions of people based on their status in life, so eventually, I ended it."

"Wow, she sounds pretty rude."

"Honestly, I don't even know if she was aware she did things like that."

"Now, it makes sense why you ended things with her, but what I don't understand is why when you first started dating her, you told her you wanted nothing serious."

"Because I didn't. However, and I did not tell Ashley this, even though I didn't want a relationship, if I really started feeling her and thought we fit well, I would have been open to things progressing."

"Sounds fair enough. Have you ever been in love with anyone?"

"Once, with a girl name Tish?"

"What happened?"

"Stupidity."

"On your part or hers?"

"Mine. I was young and didn't want anyone to "stop me from living," so I pushed her away. Being the smart lady she was, she left."

"That sucks; I'm sure you regretted that for a while."

"I did, but everything happens for a reason. What about you, any loves in your past?"

"There was one guy I loved. His name was Greg." She hesitated a little embarrassed, then added. "He was a magician."

Kody caught his laugh before it fully erupted. "Wait, don't tell me. Did he disappear?"

"He didn't, but his dick did, and it reappeared in another woman."

They shared a laugh at that one.

They continued talking about past relationships the rest of the way home. She shared more about her past hurts that caused her to take a pause from dating in the first place.

Winter was yet again reminded of how easy he was to talk to. Throughout the conversation, she had to keep telling herself that sex with him was off the table. Her body would just have to stop wanting him because she wasn't giving in. She could do this; she could be strong.

◆◆◆

She really couldn't. Fifteen minutes later, they were at her front door kissing. What started out as a sweet gesture of him seeing her to the door safely turned into a hot, erotic kissing session.
She couldn't help it, when he brushed his fingers over her cheek and thanked her again for accompanying him to the dinner, she couldn't resist. His touch always awakened something in her.

Finally pulling away, she told him she had to go because there were things she had to do in the morning. What she really meant was he was the thing she wanted to be doing until the morning.

He lifted her hand to his lips and told her he would see her tomorrow. She hurried inside because if she caught one more glimpse of him before the night was over, she would have no will power left.

Chapter 13
Winter

There was Candace. Chloe couldn't stand Candace. She had good reason, though, because Candace was always flirting with Derek when they came to the cafe. However, in Candace's defense, though, if there were such a thing, she flirted with most girls' men.

She was a wanna-be actress who had dreams of making it big in Atlanta or LA, but Winter was starting to think the only TV time Candace was going to get was when they showed her picture on the news for being murdered by a vengeful woman.

"One day, someone is going to beat her ass," Jessica said. "I wouldn't mind it being me, but my last fight was in high school. I'd probably be fighting her using the windmill arms."

Jessica backed a bit away from the table to demonstrate her, as she would call it, windmill attack.

They all laughed.

"Yeah, girl. That's pretty outdated. You might want to update your self-defense moves a bit first," Chloe said. "But I know what you mean. I'm all for avoiding violence, but she is always trying to push those buttons. Derek ignored her, and I've told her to check her "hospitality." I even mentioned her evidently too forward flirtations with the manager, but nothing. He always says he will have a talk with her."

"Makes sense; her manager is married, so she's probably sleeping with him. You know that's her only qualification," Jessica said.

"True," Winter and Chloe said in agreement.

Another waitress, with a name tag that read Brenda, came by and deposited three chicken salads on the table. It was early November, and Chloe, Jessica and Winter were at a popular cafe, by the name of UpDial, that they loved to frequent, catching up on their lunch break.

"I still can't believe I've been married for 3 months," Chloe said.

"Well, believe it, girl, cause you are! Speaking of," Jessica said, rummaging through her gigantic bag and pulling out a box that she passed to Chloe. "Mrs. Malcolm sent you this."

"Awe, Cat Lady Malcolm got us a gift? That's so sweet." Then looking at Jessica with a touch of alarm said, "Is it something I will need to have cleaned first?"

"No, don't worry. She gave me the money and told me what to buy. The gift never spent any time inside her house."

"Thank Goodness, I don't want to listen to Derek with that constant sneezing and coughing all night."

Chloe's husband, Derek, was highly allergic to cats. And as sweet as she was, Mrs. Malcom, aka Cat Lady Malcolm, had tons of them. She was a nice, highly respected woman in her seventies that lived next door to Jessica. She used to be a veterinarian who owned her own practice with her husband, Marlin.

They both loved animals, cats, especially. When Marlin passed a few years back, the only thing she had to remember him by were the two cats they owned. However, eventually, two turned to four, and then four turned to seven.

She loved those cats like they were her own children, and since she and Marlin never had kids, in a way, that's exactly what they were.

The problem with having so many cats was that there was cat hair everywhere. Unable to clean like she used to, Mrs. Malcolm hired a cleaning service to keep things in order, but that cat hair was just as much part of the home as Mrs. Malcolm herself.

She often joked that she would have sent them to a shelter for all the shedding they did if she didn't love them so much.

The first time Chloe and Derek met Mrs. Malcolm was at Jessica's house warming party. She needed help with some boxes at her place next door and Derek, offered to give her a hand. Unfortunately, getting all the boxes moved wasn't a success because Derek's allergies won out over his goodwill.

"That's great. Tell her thank you so much for thinking of us," Chloe said.

"I will," Jessica promised. "Now, back to the details of your newly married status."

Chloe beamed. "It just feels surreal sometimes. Like, I'm still that little girl thinking about someday, and someday has already happened. I truly believed you and Winter would be married before me. Specifically, you, Jessica."

"What? Why me first?" Jessica asked in disbelief.

"Oh, Jessica," Winter said. "Don't be modest. You know you are the most put-together girl we know. You like things done in order. If Married, with 2.5 kids and a white Pickett fence needed a visual, you would be it."

"Yes, maybe that's true, but my OCD hasn't won me any relationships that got me to the alter now, has it? Goes to show, life is full of unpredictable surprises. In this case, I'm glad that the surprise of happily ever after went to a dear friend of mine."

"Don't make me cry," Chloe said.

"It's true, you're a great friend, Clo. A little bat shit, but definitely a keeper."

"I second the bat shit," Winter added.

"Alright, Winter, I see how you're going to be. Let's get the spotlight off me and shift it on to you. Jessica isn't dating anyone right now, but you sure are. Tell us about Kody; he get some Winter loving yet?"

"Yes, do tell," Jessica said, taking a bite of her salad.

"Not yet, but it's getting so hard to keep telling myself no."

"What's the holdup?" Jessica asked.

"Honestly, I think it's two things. One is that I like him too much. We have so much fun together, no matter if it's going out or staying in. I have never felt this way about a guy before. It was bad enough when my relationships ended in the past, but it's different with Kody. It's like things are so good with us, I'm scared sex will ruin things. What if I do it and once again it doesn't work out? I'm scared I will really be broken this time. I'm just tired of going down the same road, you know?"

"No, I don't know. You can't live your life afraid. I'm not saying open your heart or your legs to every guy you meet, but don't let your decisions about moving forward be based on fear. You deserve to be loved, and we all know the road to real love isn't easy, so that means take your ass back down that road again and again if you have to. Unless—" she said with a pause, "this is really about that run-in with that Ashley girl from the party last month?"

"No, it's not about her. I've already determined I'm not going to judge him based on past relationships. But at this point, my ass that you spoke of is sporting permanent tire marks. I feel like I'm setting myself up if I go any further. It's only been three months, and in four more, he's gone. I'm not saying I will never attempt a relationship again but getting more involved with Kody, in particular, just doesn't seem like a good idea. No matter how bad I want to screw his brains out. And oh my goodness," she said, biting her lip, "I want to really bad."

"Wait," Chloe said. "Hasn't this man already re-piped your whole house and come to your aid with every scary nightmare you've had and hasn't once tried to push the idea of sex?"

Winter let out a small breath, nodded and then picked up her water to take a sip.

"Winter, I love you, but you're dumb as hell. If you don't give him some ass, I will," Chloe said, placing a hand on Winter's knee.

Winter almost spat her drink out. She fully caught herself just in time, and only a few beads of water escaped. Wiping her mouth and coughing, she took a minute to collect herself.

Still laughing, she said, "Girl, your crazy ass almost choked me!"

"What? It's the truth. Oh, wait, I'm married. I can't do it, so I'm going to pass the baton over to Jessica and let her do what I can't. Jessica, you got my back, right?" she said jokingly.

"Sure do. I think I can take one for the team." Jessica said.

They shared a laugh.

"Seriously, Wint," Chloe said soberly, "you know I joke a lot, but I never, ever want you to do anything that you aren't comfortable with. Having said that, Jessica is right. Don't block what could be because of past hurt. Sex aside, you like this man. I see the way you light up when you talk about him. Follow your heart and do what feels right. So what if he leaves in a few months? If it's real, it will work out.

Now, tell us the second reason you haven't slept with him?"

Winter finished chewing her bite of salad and swallowed.

"This is going to sound weird, but he makes me feel like he could fuck me senseless, and that intimidates the hell out of me. Y'all know I have never orgasmed from sex, and normally, that doesn't bother me. But liking him as much as I do, combined with my sexual inexperience, and I feel like a shy virgin all over again."

"Oh, I know what you're talking about," Chloe said. "He gives you that speak a new language vibe."

"Huh?" Jessica and Winter asked in Unison.

"The type of guy that fucks you so good he has you saying shit that you don't even know what it means?"

"That's the type," Winter said.

Then they all started laughing again.

After finishing lunch and saying their goodbyes, Winter arrived back at work with a clearer head. Walking into the building, she pulled her button-up sweater a little tight.

The early November air offered a slight chill that Winter delighted in. Falling in line with her name, she did love the colder season. Entering the building, she noticed that there were fewer people around than before she went to lunch.

"Hey, Winter," Gary called, heading in her direction.

He was the Production Assistant to a well-known director who was currently filming the sequel to a highly anticipated horror flick.

"Hey, Gary, what's up?"

"Please, tell me your day isn't too busy? We need a hand with staging to finish up a scene. Five people called out sick today and two more headed home during lunchtime. This damn bug going around is putting us so far behind."

"I don't think I'm too busy. Let me just put my purse and sweater in my office, and I'll be right over."

"Thank you," Gary said, clasping his hands together and shaking them emphatically.

Winter dropped off her belongings and headed back to help with the setup. It was different being on this side of the work. She always helped out when she could, but with inventory and managing staff being so busy, she couldn't always help much with the physical labor of creating the magic. But she enjoyed the work.

The flu traveling its way through the studio was a common occurrence this time of year. The constant hacking and coughing was almost like background noise everyone expected.

It dawned on Winter that she hadn't seen Lisa all day. Before lunch, she was busy making sure she got things done so that she could have a longer lunch break with the girls. When she was done helping Gary's team set up, she would find Lisa to make sure she was ok.

"You want this over there?" Jeff, one of the setup team members, asked, holding up a square glass cube.

"Yeah. Make sure that it is located closest to the right of the table. It needs to be in the shot because I think it's going to be knocked over by 'accident.'"

"Ok, got it."

She leaned over to resume, setting up the artificial plants. This scene was in an office. Some crooked lawyer was about to meet his doom if she recalled correctly.

Her mind drifted back to Kody. The things she could do with him on that desk. She imagined him towering over her as they tore at each other's clothes, consumed by her desire for him to be inside her.

A cough behind her made her turn around.

It was Lisa. She looked horrible. "Lisa, are you ok?"

Lisa shook her head. "It's this damn flu. I guess I'm its latest victim," she said in a congested voice. "I dragged myself out of bed because I had to finish some work in another area that I promised you would get done, but now I'm so weak I can't even work up the strength to masturbate when I get home tonight."

Winter started laughing, then said, "Aw, poor baby. You're about to head home now, though, right?" It was more of a statement than a question.

Coughing and taking a moment to catch her breath, Lisa nodded.

"Good. Thank you so much for coming in, sweetie. Is there anything I can do for you?" Winter asked.

"Would you like the flu? I'll give you mine."

"No. I think I'm good."

Lisa turned to go and then stopped. "Oh yeah," she said, then paused to cough several more times. "Mr. Sanders is out too. He left about an hour ago. He said something to the effect of his "nasals leaking noodles" or some odd gibberish only he understands and went home. I assumed it was in reference to his runny nose."

"Yeah, that sounds like him. Thanks for telling me. You get some rest, drink plenty of water and skip the masturbation for a few days, and I'll check on you later."

Lisa dragged herself out of the staging area, and Winter got back to it. With everyone around her getting sick, she hoped that she could avoid being next, but she suspected she wouldn't be so lucky.

Within the next few days, her predictions proved true. What started out as a scratchy throat on Monday manifested into a full-blown cough with congestion and constant sneezing by Wednesday. She forced herself to do one more day of work because Lisa and Mr. Sanders, although better, weren't completely out of the woods yet. They would take a couple of more days before they returned. In the meantime, they were doing as much as they could from home as it pertained to their respective roles.

Winter was pushing herself to try and make it until the end of the week, but when she woke up with body aches and a fever Thursday morning, she had to surrender to the sickness.

Coughing and shivering uncontrollably, she made her way to the kitchen to get some tea. She didn't have much of an appetite and felt very weak. Aware that she hadn't been feeling well the past couple of days, Kody came by to check on her.

She tried to beg him not to, but he kept insisting, and she was too out of it to push back. As she laid in bed, wearing three layers of clothes and covered up to her neck in blankets, Kody sat beside her on the bed, asking what he could do for her.

"You should go before I get you sick," she croaked out

"Don't worry about me, Winter." Nodding his head in the direction of her nightstand, he said, "I put you some water, juice and lozenges right there. I got the key you left for me on the counter, so I can drop off your medicine, and of course, I will keep my cell on me if you need to contact me. Are you sure you don't need anything else?"

She weakly shook her head.

"Get some rest, and I'll be back after work." He kissed her on her forehead. His lips felt warm and smooth on her achy skin. She closed her eyes for just a moment intending to blink but unexpectedly fell asleep.

The next morning, she awoke, still feeling bad. She couldn't believe she had slept all the way through the previous day. She heard some moving around in the kitchen and assumed it was Kody.

She went into the bathroom to wash her face and brush her teeth, then she made the slow, painful walk to the kitchen.

"Hi," he said, coming over to give her a gentle hug. "How are you feeling?"

"Still not the best. What are you up to?"

"I was making you some soup. I know you still probably aren't hungry, but it's for when you are."

She smiled, then coughed. "That's nice of you, especially since you don't cook. Will it make me worse?"

"You got jokes," he said. "No, it will not make you worse, and remember, I said I don't have much time to cook. I very well know *how* to cook."

"I'm already sick; what's the worse you could do?" she said.

Coming around to the table where she was sitting, he said. "I am so glad you took time out of your schedule to come and poke fun at me, but you should be resting. I'm about to go back to get some stuff done at the warehouse while the guys work on the house. Would you like to be set up out here on the couch or back in bed?"

She pointed to the couch, and he helped her get set up, bringing all the things she would need and placing them on the coffee table. Then he brought her extra blankets and pillows to the couch.

"The soup is in the fridge whenever you are ready to eat."

She looked up at him. "Thank you so much, Kody. I appreciate everything."

"No problem, Winter," he said, giving her that sexy smile she had grown to love. If she wasn't so weak, she would be all over him.

"Before I go, I'd meant to ask you why you never park in your garage?"

Picking up her tea to take a sip, she said, "it stopped working like eight months ago. I hadn't had the chance to get someone to come out here and fix it. I better do it soon because it's getting colder, and it would be nice to not have to go outside to get in my car."

"I was thinking the same thing," he said, "Which is why I fixed it. You can park in there now. Call me if you need me." Then he turned and left.

"Hell yeah," she thought. "It's final, he's getting some."

◆◆◆

A few days later, she felt much better. It was Monday night, and she and Kody were sitting at the table, playing Monopoly. She still hadn't fully regained her appetite, so she was eating popcorn and drinking juice.

The soup Kody had made was delicious. It was the only actual meal she had eaten over the last few days. She had finished the last of it that morning, and because she enjoyed it so much, he offered to make her more, and she accepted.

"Why do you have more money than me? I think you're cheating, Kody. Taking from the sick is not a good look."

"It's not my fault you didn't buy the railroads. I told you, you can't be caught sleeping on the railroads."

She rolled again and ended up landing on some property he owned. Silently holding out his hand for the money, she squinted at him and then gave him what was owed. He picked up the dice and took his turn.

"This is fun. Why don't you tell me more funny stories about your childhood before this NyQuil I took kicks in?"

Kody thought a moment, then his lips curved in a smile.

"You see this scar right here?" He was pointing on the side of his jaw. Winter leaned towards him and spotted it. She had never noticed it before.

"I see it."

"I got it when I was ten and, at the time, I told everyone at school it was from a pit bull that attacked me out of nowhere, and I managed to escape. But that is not how I got it. The truth is, I was a Michael Jackson fan, or more like fanatic. I wanted to learn how to dance like him so bad. I practiced for hours at a time, trying to master the moonwalk. One day, I was really feeling confident and decided I could probably figure it out if I had a stage to perform it on. So, way too sure of myself, I went to the dining room, cleared everything off the table and climbed up. Everything was going fine until I decided that I should do a spin at the end of my moonwalk performance, and I fell and busted my ass, as well as my chin falling off the table."

Winter's lips twitched, and she covered her mouth with her hand.

"You can laugh," he said, already laughing himself.

She started cracking up. "I'm sorry. Why didn't you just use the floor?"

"I was ten. I was an idiot. In my mind, the floor was not a stage."

Catching her breath, Winter said, "You know what? I'm laughing at you, and I had something similar happen to me. I wanted desperately to have those crinkle curls that were so popular, but my mom refused to buy me the curling tool for it. So I used the one bulky curly iron I had to try and create the crinkle effect. I ended up burning my neck and told all my friends it was a hickey."

"A hickey? A hickey doesn't look like a burn mark."

"I know! But we were like eleven, I think, and truly nerdy. We had never seen a hickey up close. Even if one of my friends thought I was lying, they never called me out on it. It's not like they'd ever had one to compare it to."

Shaking his head, he said. "Well, I hope you eventually got one so that you could see just how off base you were."

"You know what?" she said, thinking about it. "A guy has never given me a hickey, but they've also never given me an orgasm, so I guess I'm two for two."

As soon as it came out, she wanted to take it back. She didn't mean to say that. She was feeling way too relaxed, and it just slipped out.

"Damn you, NyQuil," she thought.

She was sure he was about to give her some cheesy come-on line. When they found out, most guys couldn't wait to start promising her endless nights of world-rocking sex and orgasms. Which is why she had begun to avoid mentioning it. She looked up at him.

"It's your roll," he said.

She picked up the dice. Maybe he didn't hear her, or maybe he didn't know what to say. That was an odd thing being in her thirties and never experienced an orgasm from a guy. It could have just weirded him out, and he didn't want to embarrass her.

They continued playing the game a few more rounds. Still, he said nothing. The silence was killing her. She might regret hearing what he thought, but she had to know.

"So, you aren't going to say anything?" Winter asked.

"About what?" he said, moving his tiny sliver top hat the appropriate spaces.

"About what I said."

"I don't know, Winter, I'm not really into it?"

"Not into it? You mean you've never done that for a girl before."

"I have, but it isn't really my thing."

"*What in the hell!*" she thought. "*What type of selfish man didn't like to give women orgasms.*"

Collecting herself, she said, "So you get yours, but you're not interested in them getting theirs?"

"Honestly, they don't even have to give me one."

Feeling as if the NyQuil had to be affecting her hearing and comprehension, she asked, "Kody, what are you talking about?"

"I'm talking about hickeys. What are you talking about?"

"Orgasms!" she said louder than she intended.

"Oh, those," he said, still sounding nonchalant. "I can give you one of those, but I draw the line at hickeys."

Then he looked up with a mischievous grin on his face. Winter started laughing and threw a piece of popcorn at him. He dodged it and started laughing too.

Chapter 14
Winter

The following weekend, Winter was ready to get out and have some fun. Being cooped up in the house, sick and feeling like death's play toy had made her really want to live. Kody thought it would be a good idea to go bowling.

They had previously gone as just the two of them, so this time, they figured adding more people would spice up the competition.

Kody invited Jackson and Erica, and Winter invited Jessica, Chloe and Derek. Jessica refusing to be, as she called it, "the lonely wheel," invited a male friend to help even the numbers.

The outing also offered an opportunity for an official meet and greet between Winter's people and Kody's. Plus, Winter had only spent time with Jackson and Erica briefly at the company event in October. They seemed like a fun couple, so she was looking forward to more time with them.

When everyone arrived at the bowling alley, introductions and warm greetings were exchanged and received. Once they had been assigned a lane, Winter headed to the restroom room, and Jessica and Chloe decided to tag along. Erica was at the bar area, ordering everyone drinks, and the guys were doing some sort of male bonding over an upcoming football game.

As soon as they were inside the bathroom, Chloe said, "Damn, Winter. I see why you're all hot and bothered. That man is sexy as hell."

"I have to agree. Do you think he would mind being cloned?" Jessica asked.

"I'll have to ask," Winter responded jokingly.

They finished up and prepared to exit the bathroom to rejoin the rest of their party.

Before they did, Chloe halted Winter and said, "by the way, you are right, that man will fuck you senseless; I know the type when I see them. But you'll be fine. You're just tall enough to ride that ride." Then she slapped Winter on the ass and caught up to Jessica.

It was a joyous, competitive, exciting night. They played two games, and each round was the guys against the girls. The guys won the first round, girls won the second.

Demanding a tie-breaker round because Erica and Chloe were certain that Jackson and Derek were in cahoots because they kept distracting them every time they went up to throw the ball, they played a third game.

When the guys won again, the girls threw in the towel but promised a rematch on a day when the alcohol wasn't getting to them.

Winter wholeheartedly enjoyed her night. Kody seemed to like her friends, and she could tell they liked him as well. He fit in so easily with his jokes and laid back personality.

She also solidified her first impression of Jackson and Erica. They were such a great couple who loved to laugh, have a good time, and were just as silly as her group of friends. Erica was a great bowler and talked as much trash as Chloe did.

On the way home, Kody verbally stated what she already knew—that he'd had a great time and enjoyed getting to know her other halves. They ended the night in front of the fireplace at her house, kissing and cuddling.

The next day, they decided to go out again. She didn't feel like making dinner, and there was a new gourmet pizza place she wanted to try out.

Upon entering the restaurant, she could already tell that she would love this place. It had a cozy look with an indoor brick fireplace, spacious wooden booths and various pizza creations on display. Winter couldn't wait to eat. Her appetite had returned with a vengeance after she got well, and she was starving.

Their waitress was a girl named Bianca, who looked to be in her mid-twenties. She was friendly enough, actually a little too friendly.

Every time Kody asked something, she seemed to linger on her response and make additional suggestions, but when Winter asked her a question, she would just answer straight away—no further discussion, and barely made eye contact.

The actions were obvious enough to be understood but subtle enough to make Winter look like a madwoman for getting snappy with her. If Kody noticed, he didn't say anything.

However, he repeatedly placed his hand on Winter's and deferred to her whenever Bianca asked him a question.

Finally, after deciding on a large pizza with extra marinara sauce, tons of vegetables, pepperoni, ground beef and extra cheese, they handed "Bitchanca," as Winter had mentally named her, their menus and settled in.

Scanning the room, Winter noticed the place wasn't too crowded, which made sense with it being a Sunday night. Most people were probably at home getting ready for work, getting kids to bed or watching football. She wondered if they'd make it home in time to catch the end of the game.

Touching the pocket of her jacket that was hung on the back of her chair, she realized she'd left her phone in the car.

"What time is it?" she asked.

Kody stretched out his arm and checked his watch. "Around 7:30."

"Good. I'm hoping we can catch at least the end of the game."

"We should be able to," he said.

"That's a nice watch," she said, admiring the dome-shaped accessory with its unique layers of gold and blue. "Who makes it?"

He glanced at it again. "This one is by Audemars Piguet."

"Never heard of them."

"It's a Swiss luxury watchmaker. I got into watches because of my dad. He collected really nice ones, and I think it kinda rubbed off on me. Shortly after he passed, I remember seeing this one in a store when I was in Paris, and I had to have it. It was one I knew he would have loved. I remember when I was a kid, and I'd ask him why he likes watches so much. Without fail, he'd always say, a man only has so much time on his hands, use it wisely and remember that as long as time keeps counting, you have no room for doubting."

"That sounds like a nice memory. Did he ever officially come out and tell you what he meant? Although I'm sure you eventually drew your own conclusions."

Kody smiled to himself, obviously taken back to a different period in his life.

"My dad liked to make everything a teaching moment. When I was a kid, it confused the mess out of me. I would keep saying, "but dad, time doesn't do math," in reference to the counting part. He'd just smile and say, "no, son, but it's always adding up." When I was older, I finally understood that he was saying life will always keep moving, so you shouldn't waste a second of it doubting yourself or living in fear. It was that piece of advice that helped me take the leap and start my own business."

She touched his face. "Your dad sounded like a very wise man; he would be so proud of you."

He leaned over and kissed her then.

"Thank you," he said.

When their pizza arrived. It was every bit as delicious as Winter assumed it would be. Gourmet was certainly the right name for the type of pizza they served. It all tasted so fresh and savory, she ended up eating four slices right along with Kody.

Fully satiated and happy, they waited for the check. When it arrived, Winter reached for it.

"Nope," Kody said, beating her to it and sliding it in front of him.

"Kody, I never pay when we go out. Let me pay at least this time. You're kinda killing me with all the kindness here."

"You'll live," he said, placing his card into the black check booklet and sliding it towards the edge of the table.

Almost immediately, Bitchanca came back over to get it.

"Thank you," Winter said to Kody.

"No problem."

She appreciated everything he had done. She wanted to do something nice for him, but that was hard because he never let her pay when he was around. Even still, she had to give him something as a token of her appreciation.

Chloe would suggest sex, which was a given at this point, but she also wanted to give him a gift. She had been trying to think of something for months but kept drawing a blank.

Suddenly she thought of it—the perfect gift. So perfect, in fact, it would also solve the gift dilemma she had been facing for Mr. Sanders's niece.

They heard the melody of Kody's phone ringing. He pulled it out of his pocket, checked the screen and put it to his ear.

"Hey," he said. "No, I didn't. Did you need me too?"

He waited for a moment, then said, "Repeat that."

After another pause, "Jackson, I'm sorry I can barely hear you. Hold on one second. I'll step outside to see if I can hear you better."

Pulling the phone away from his ear, he said to Winter. "Do you mind excusing me for a second?"

"Of course not."

"Thanks, I'll be right back."

He headed toward the exit door just as the waitress was approaching to pick up the check.

A few minutes later, Bitchanca returned with the black book that contained what she assumed was Kody's card and the receipt. She placed it on the table, told Winter to have a nice night and practically skipped away.

Winter rolled her eyes and reached for her water. In doing so, she accidentally knocked the book off the table. Leaning over to pick it up, she saw it had opened and a card fell out.

The card read.

"If you need a reservation or anything else next time, call me" and went on to include a phone number and below it, Bianca Reynolds.

Winter was pissed, and Bitchanca had just lost the "anca" and was now simply Bitch. Winter didn't even like that word. She rarely used it and hated referring to other women that way, but in this case, the title was so fitting it practically wrote itself.

She couldn't believe the guts Bitch had. It didn't matter that she and Kody weren't actually together. Bitch didn't know that!

She was right on the edge of calling the waitress back over and giving her a piece of her mind, but then it dawned on her there was something she actually wanted more… to see what Kody would do.

She liked him and was finally ready to have sex with him and then this happens. Was it a sign to test him? Would he take the card? There was really only one way to find out.

In truth, she couldn't be mad if he took the card; he was not hers, although her heartfelt otherwise. Pushing her feelings aside, she put the card back into the book and laid it on the table.

A few minutes later, Kody returned. "I'm sorry it took longer than I expected. You ready to go?"

"Sure," she said.

He grabbed the booklet and opened it. Trying not to be too obvious, she pulled on her sweater and started buttoning it while discreetly watching him out of her peripheral. He hesitated a moment. It wasn't a long moment, and the only reason she noticed it was because she knew to look for it.

Bracing herself for his reaction, she saw him retrieve his card, a copy of the receipt and nothing more. He closed the book and put it back on the table. Then he looked up and smiled at her, extended his hand and said, "shall we?"

◆◆◆

They were in the car now, and she kept peaking glances at him.

"Could he get any sexier?!"

She wanted him bad. Very bad. She wanted him now. But being Kody, she knew he wouldn't try anything without her giving him the green light. How could she push him? She didn't want to just come out and say it. With other men, she would have, but Kody somehow made her feel like it was her first time all over again. In a way, maybe it was. It had been well over a year after all.

Hoping to create an in, she said, "Does that happen to you a lot? Women practically throwing themselves at you?"

She already knew he would know what she was referring to, even though he didn't know she had seen the card. The gutsy waitress was far too obvious in actions alone.

"Sometimes," he said.

"How often do you accept the offer?"

"It used to be often, now not so much."

"Why is that?" Recalling a previous conversation, she said, "oh wait, I remember you said that you've grown out of that."

"You would be correct."

"But don't you miss it?"

"Random sex? Not really. Don't get me wrong, I love sex. BUT, at some point, you want a relationship to be about more than…"

"Sex," she said, finishing his sentence. "I completely understand that."

"Exactly," he responded. "But speaking of sex, I remember you telling me that a guy has never given you an orgasm before. That sounds like a much more interesting topic; let's elaborate on that."

She shifted uncomfortably in her seat, but she wasn't backing down. "Ok, what do you want to know?"

"First, I have to clarify, have you ever been able to give yourself an orgasm?"

"Yes."

"But you've never had an orgasm through sex?"

"Sadly, never."

"Oral?"

"Nope. But I haven't met many guys that are willing to do that."

"Interesting."

"Why interesting?"

"You said you haven't met a lot of guys that are into that."

"I haven't. They want you to do it to them, but that's kinda where it ends. What's your stance? Are you that type?"

"Are you asking if I'm the type of guy that eats pussy?"

His question caught her off guard as it was bold and direct. She found herself squeezing her legs together to provide some relief to the throbbing happening in between her thighs. She felt anxious and even more turned on.

She cleared her throat. "Yeah," she said, trying to sound more relaxed than she did.

"Do you want me to be?"

"Here's my chance," she thought.

"Maybe," she said aloud.

"What the hell, Winter!" she mentally scolded herself. "The answer was supposed to be yeah… fuck yeah."

He chuckled. "That wasn't a definitive answer, but it'll do. Have you ever gotten close to an orgasm during sex?"

"Honestly, I don't think so."

"Why didn't you just tell them that you weren't satisfied? Maybe they could have tried something new."

"I don't know. I guess it seems a little cruel. I'm sure the guy might have been doing the best he could, and here I go crushing his ego."

Deciding to go a step further to gauge his reaction and hopefully find the courage she seems to misplace every time the topic of sex comes up, she said, "I mean, imagine if we were together and I had to say hey Kody, you're not getting me there. Wouldn't that be horrible?"

He glanced at her for a moment, then looked back at the road. "If you don't want me to pull this truck over right now, you may want to avoid using me in your hypotheticals."

Smiling, she said, "I'm sorry, was that rude?"

"Not at all," he said cooly. "I just don't like being an example in your sexual failures."

"It was just a little joke, no need to get all sensitive. Unless I'm hitting on a bit of truth. Maybe you can't satisfy a woman either?" she teased.

She wanted to push him. She needed him to pull over right now and fulfill this desire she had been trying to fight since she first met him.

"Would you like me to solve your curiosity?"

She felt the tingling in between her legs jump several notches and her stomach tighten. She was beyond ready.

"What if I am? I'm not afraid of you pulling this truck over."

She sat really still waiting for his reply, his eagerness, his...something, but he didn't say anything.

"Did you hear me?" she said.

"I heard you," he responded. He drove another few minutes and then signaled to pull over.

Her heart rate sped up.

"Was this really about to happen? Had she made a mistake? Should she have waited until they got home? "

Questions consumed her mind. Not sure of the answers, but sure she wanted him, she looked over at him.

Once he put the car in park, he hit the button to release his seatbelt and then did the same to hers.

It immediately retracted, freeing her to lean further up in her seat. Meeting her the rest of the way, he touched her face and then traced his thumb over her lips.

"So, finally, you are ready to let me touch you," he said, then kissed her on the lips.

"To taste you," he said, kissing her again.

"And be inside you?"

All she could do was nod as he slowly and sweetly started kissing her again. He parted her lips with his tongue, and she moaned into his mouth. She felt her whole body go weak. He moved down to her neck, and she tilted her head back and began rubbing her hands up and down his back.

It was feeling so good, and she was already so turned on. She had to get closer to him.

As if he read her mind, he leaned in more towards her and wrapped one arm around her waist, then resumed laying soft, heated kisses up and down her neck and collar bone.

Out of nowhere, he stopped. When she opened her eyes, she saw him pulling her seatbelt back around her and then clicking it into the latch.

Still, only inches away from her lips, he said, "I'm all for spontaneity, but after that little joke you made, sex in a truck where space and time limit what I plan to do to you, is letting you off the hook easy and that's not going to happen."

Then he re-latched his seat belt, put the car in drive and got back on the road.

She stared straight ahead for the longest time and thought to herself.

"Damn. I'm fucked."

Chapter 15
Kody

"STOP BREAKING MY HEART, FALCONS," Winter yelled at the TV.

She turned her back on the TV, grabbed her bottle of beer from the coffee table and took a large gulp. It was Thursday evening, and they were watching an entertaining, competitive game of football.

They had just finished eating dinner. Braised short ribs, with rice and green beans, and as usual, decided to finish the rest of the game in front of the TV.

Amused with her tantrum-like behavior that consisted of adorable pouting and animated stomping, Kody decided to add fuel to the fire and said, "What did you expect when you picked a horrible team to be a fan of?"

"Oh really?" she said, turning in his direction and placing her hands on her hips.

"Yup," Kody said, taking a sip of his own beer.

"Well, Mr. Benton, would you like to put your money where your mouth is?"

Kody placed his beer on the coffee table and met her gaze. "I would love to. What do you have in mind?"

"Just a little bet. I mean, if you can handle it."

"I think I can handle betting against a team that is likely to give my team an easy win."

"Watch it, buddy," she said, pointing at him. "So, here's the deal. If they win this game tonight, you have to do whatever I want. No complaints, no back outs and no hesitation. And if you win, I'll abide by the same guidelines."

"You sure you want to place that bet? They are already down by 12."

"Yes, I do," she said, holding her chin high. "I have faith in my team."

"Alright," he said. "What would you want?"

Thinking, Winter looked around the house, tapping her finger to her lips.

"I got it! If I win, you have to go antique shopping with me. And I'm not just talking a couple of hours, in and out. I mean a whole day from location to location, with a stop at my favorite restaurant downtown for lunch."

"I can agree to that."

"Good," she said excitedly. "And what would you want?"

Kody picked up his beer and took another sip. Placing it back on the table, he said, "dessert."

Winter looked puzzled. "Just dessert, really? Wow, you're easy to please. But whatever, it's your choice. So what are you thinking? Cakes, cookies, pies?"

"I'll let you know."

"Alright, then. Come to think of it, that's weird that in all the cooking I've done for you, I have never made you dessert."

"I won't hold it against you," he said.

Winter returned to her seat on the couch. The fire was crackling, and the house was nice and warm.

He loved seeing her like this. She was so lively and cheerful. Wearing her red and black Falcons jersey with black shorts and red fuzzy footie socks, she showed her team spirit. It was in stark contrast to his basic gray sweats and sweater.

He didn't really have a favorite team; he just loved a good game. If the Falcons won, he was happy to take his loss with a smile, but if they lost… well, he had something tasty in mind.

They watched the rest of the game on the edge of their seats. Winter probably more nervous about the outcome than Kody.

When the final touchdown had been made, ensuring that the Falcons weren't going to be able to reclaim victory. Winter picked up the remote and hit the off button.

"Damn Falcons," she said. Then turning to Kody with gritted teeth, "Congratulations on your win. What type of dessert would you like?"

Kody laughed out loud. "Well, don't be so happy about it."

"Sorry," Winter said. "I just hate losing. Of course, I'd be happy to take my loss and give you what you won fair and square."

He gave her a look and then picked up his beer.

"There you go again; what was that look?"

"What look?"

"Don't play innocent with me."

Pretending he didn't know, he said. "I have no idea, Winter. I was just thinking about dessert."

"Good then, you know what you want?"

"Yes, I do," he said. "But I'll let you know for sure tomorrow."

"Works for me."

With the topic settled, Kody remembered it was something else he was supposed to ask Winter about.

"I know it's months away, but what do you think of going to Jackson's for the Super Bowl? Erica is an early planner, so she's already hounding me about attending and bringing you with me."

"Hell, yeah. I'd love to go. Jackson and Erica are a lot of fun, and I'll bet they will do a better job of cheering on the Falcons on with me, assuming they make it to the Super Bowl of course."

It made him feel good that the three of them got along so well. Seeing the happy family dynamic gave him even more of a reason to consider his future with Winter.

He still hadn't decided if he wanted to permanently relocate to Georgia, but he knew for sure that he wanted to be with her, long-distance or not. They hadn't discussed relationships, but he already felt like she belonged to him and vice versa.

She had opened up a whole lot since they first met, but he knew she still had a long way to go. He was content to continue allowing her to let him know when she was ready for the next step, and he'd take it from there.

A few days ago, on their way home from having dinner at a local pizza place, she had made it known that she was ready for sex. Part of him wanted to jump at the chance. He wanted her so bad it was hard to concentrate sometimes.

But there was no way he was going to let his first time with her be in his truck—not after that slick little comment she made.

He was Kody Fucking Benton. Even the mere idea that he couldn't satisfy a woman had no business in the same sentence with his name. No, he had a better idea that was already playing out quite nicely.

Winter was walking past him taking her beer bottle to the kitchen. As she walked by, Kody grabbed her arm and pulled her down into his lap. He kissed her deeply and passionately. He loved kissing her and how her body responded to him. He was falling in love with her. He knew it, and he welcomed it.

"What was that for?" she said.

"I'm getting ready to head home."

"Awe, really? You can stay the night if you want to."

"I would, but have some paperwork to finish up at home and a meeting with a possible new client tomorrow."

"I thought Jackson took all the meetings?"

"Jackson takes *most* of the meetings. This client wants more in-depth details about the stages of construction as it will pertain to his contract, and that is my area of expertise."

"I know another thing you're an expert in," she said, touching his lips with her fingers.

"What's that?"

"Kissing," she said and pulled him close and placed her lips on his.

◆◆◆

The next morning, Kody stood in the living room, looking around while his team members tackled projects from all sides. It was coming along quickly. He had been living there for around four and a half months, and tons of things had been checked off the list.

They had already fixed the roof, added a skylight and updated the kitchen, replaced both the front porch and back deck, replaced all the windows, removed two walls, and changed the design of the fireplace.

The owner had only requested a few changes and relied on Haven Construction to decide on anything else necessary to modernize the home. To make the home more desirable, Kody researched homes in the area to determine what features were expected and which ones would add icing on the cake to entice a prospective buyer into making an offer.

Walking into the master bath, it was barely recognizable. It looked so different compared to the original design. The plan was to add space to it by removing one wall and completely change up the look.

So far, they had relocated the plumbing, created the frame for the soaker tub and started the base for the shower.

As Kody started building the shower frame on top of the base, he was glad construction work felt so natural to him. His body was so used to it, it was as if he did the work almost robotically.

If it weren't for his extreme familiarity with what he was doing, he might have made some mistakes because his mind wasn't completely on the job. He couldn't get a sexually shy but otherwise highly confident woman off his mind.

Thinking of her reminded him that he needed to check and see when he scheduled the concrete truck to come by. This house needed a brand new driveway, and at the same time, he planned to fix a small pocket of damage to Winter's walkway.

He noticed the concrete was raised, and he wanted to repair it and then surprise her when she came home one day.

His phone rang.

"Hi, Jackson, what's up?"

"I wanted to know what time you had the meeting with the new potential today?"

"It's at five. Everything all good?"

"Yeah. I'm writing down the details of all the meetings we have set for this month. You know, because I like to keep records of all the who, what, why, when and where in case I need to refer back to it for something.

"I know how meticulous you are with the details. By the way, how does 8:30 sound for a phone conference tonight to go over the meeting?

"Sounds perfect to me. Before I go, did you ask Winter about the Super Bowl?"

"I sure did, and she said yes."

"Thank God, now Erica can leave me the hell alone."

Kody laughed.

"I swear, Kody, I love that woman, but she will stress the hell out of me when she wants something done."

"I believe you."

"Anyway, I have to go. I'm looking to see if we need to hire a few more guys in California. Work has increased for the fourth month in a row up there. Not to mention they might end up being a boss short soon, I hope."

Jackson was hinting at Kody settling down in Georgia, yet again.

"What the hell?" Kody thought. *"I'll throw him a bone."*

"They just might, Jackson. Georgia is looking pretty good to me these days."

"Thank you, Winter," Jackson yelled into the phone as if she could hear him next door. "Alright, little cousin, I'll take your almost yes and get off this phone before you have too much time to think about it," he said and hung up.

◆◆◆

Driving to his meeting, Kody decided to give Winter a call. He couldn't get her off his mind and needed to hear her voice.

"How was your day?" he asked.

"It was great. Busy, but not stressful. I have to go in early tomorrow, so I think I'm going to eat a quick bite, watch a little TV and then get ready for bed."

He glanced at the dashboard readout that displayed 4:30.

"What time do you think you'll be going to sleep?"

"Around 8:30. Why you want to come see me?" she said in a playful tone.

"I wish, sweetie. But I'll try to call you before you go to sleep."

"I'd like that. That way, I'll be sure to have sweet dreams. Good luck with your meeting."

"Thanks, gorgeous," he said, ending the call.

He hoped this wouldn't take long. This client had plans for creating a new housing community on the north side of Atlanta and was very interested in hiring Haven Construction to build it.

They'd already spoken to Jackson but wanted to see and ask more questions about plans, materials, details of each stage, etc.

Kody was happy to answer any questions they may have, but he knew the whole meeting was more of a formality. They had already stated that they would be signing the contract at their meeting with Kody today.

Arriving at the restaurant, Kody was given a ticket for Valet parking and went inside to be seated. The client arrived five minutes early, ready to hear all about the plans and give Kody insight on their new community vision.

Satisfied with Kody's responses and 100% certain that they wanted Haven Construction to handle their building needs, they signed the contract, ending the meeting.

The entire exchange took close to two hours. Kody was back in his car by seven. He was glad that his work was done for the day because he only had one thing on his mind… Winter. He imagined her wearing one of those cute pajama sets, with her hair in the messy, curly ponytail she always wore to bed.

Glancing at the clock, he figured he could get to her house by 7:30 because he had a meeting with Jackson at 8:30. His plan was simple, really. He needed her, and he would have her.

❖❖❖

Arriving at her door in just under thirty minutes, he rang the doorbell. Within seconds he heard her say, "Who is it?" from the other side of the door.

"Kody," he said.

She opened the door, and he saw the excitement followed by confusion on her face.

"I thought you said you couldn't stop by tonight. Is everything ok?"

Walking inside, he said. "Yeah, everything is fine. I just wanted to surprise you."

He pulled her to him for a kiss.

Her house was warm and always had a fresh, clean type scent in the air. She was wearing blue pajama shorts and a matching shirt that read, *"Sleep is my hobby."*

"I love seeing your pajamas," he said, pointing at the shirt.

"Thanks. But look at you all GQ and sexy in your black suit. Can I get you anything?"

"No, I'm fine."

"Did you get the contract?"

"Yeah, we did."

"Congratulations, Kody!"

"Thanks, but it's no big deal."

"It kinda is," she said. "Another contract means more money. What business doesn't want that?"

"I'm good on money," he said, leaning on the door frame to the living room.

"Arrogant much?"

"I'm not being arrogant, just stating a fact."

"Most people aren't so que sera, sera about gaining more money for their company. Kinda makes a person wonder..." she said, trailing off.

He tilted his head. "Is there a question in there somewhere?"

He knew she would never ask him about his income. Not that he'd hide it from her if she did. But asking questions like that just didn't fit with her.

"Not one that I'm willing to ask," she said.

He smiled at her. "You are so fucking sexy, do you know that?"

In response, she smiled and then bit her lip as if the compliment made her nervous.

His need for her intensified then. Her lip-biting turned him on beyond measure. Straightening so that he was no longer against the door frame, he said, "Millions is the answer to your unasked question."

Then, he walked into the living room towards the kitchen table. When he got there, he removed his suit jacket, placed it on the back of the chair and sat down.

"Why don't you come sit down?" he said to her.

He could see the anxiety growing in her eyes. She didn't know what to expect, and he liked it that way.

"Umm, is there something you wanted to talk about?"

"Not particularly," he responded.

"You sure you don't want something to drink?" she said, seeming to try and buy time.

"I'm fine. Come sit," he repeated.

Winter

Something was up. She could tell, but what? Was he finally about to tell her that he had a girlfriend back in California? A long lost kid? Oh no, an STD?!

But he didn't seem like he came to deliver bad news, plus she asked him if he wanted to talk, and he said no.

Cautiously, she walked to the table while he followed her with his eyes. She couldn't read him. She hated when he did that. Made his face blank, and she had to freak out on the inside like some awkward teenager unsure of herself.

Those looks unnerved her and turned her on all at once. It was annoying how sexy he looked sitting there confidently with his arms crossed, watching her.

As she approached the table, she reached out to grab the chair next to him and began to pull it out.

"No," he said quietly but sternly and placed a finger on top of the table in front of him.

She laughed nervously. "You mean sit on the table, seriously?"

In response, he just lifted a brow.

"He isn't going to do what I'm thinking, is he? He wouldn't. He couldn't... I shouldn't."

"C'mon, Kody. I don't know if..."

"Winter, stop stalling. I can't satisfy a woman, remember? So you have nothing to fear."

Oh, he was good! He was going to make her eat those words while he basically ate.. even the thought made her wet.

Maybe he was just bluffing. Yeah, that was it. He was just seeing how far he could push her.

Finding some courage, because she wouldn't let this demure woman he seemed to spark in her run things, she stepped forward and got up on the table to sit in front of him.

"Now what?" She said.

Saying nothing, he leaned forward and put his hand around each thigh, and pulled her closer to him. Then he said, "up."

Winter complied, and he pulled off her pajama shorts and underwear in one smooth motion.

Spreading her legs. He slowly started kissing her inner left thigh as he massaged and caressed the other.

Winter's brain was screaming. *"This isn't real. He isn't going to do this. But it feels real. Oh, so real."*

As he was making his way towards her main event, Winter braced herself for the pleasure she would feel, but instead of kissing her there, he kissed upward, on to her stomach and laid a trail of kissing over to her other thigh.

Her breathing was increasing. She didn't know how she could be so tense yet so ready at the same time. Once again, Kody slowly started moving his mouth towards her sex.

He glided his tongue over her pussy, wrapped his hand around each thigh and opened her legs wider. She didn't protest. She wanted him to have full access to do anything he pleased.

The wetness of his tongue felt so good. She could feel herself getting wetter, and Kody's gentle licks became firmer as he started sucking around and then directly on her clitoris.

Dizzy with pleasure, she grabbed the side of the table for support and instinctively arched her back.

"Where did he learn to do this?" she thought. "Is he doing that alphabet tracing thing I've always heard about? Or writing some complicated math equation?"

Whatever it was, it felt amazing and was causing her to shake and moan uncontrollably.

Without thinking, she heard herself say, "Don't stop."

Obviously, with no intention of stopping, Kody continued tasting her. After a moment, she felt him slide a finger in. The jolt of pleasure made her jump back. But already anticipating her move, Kody had placed his opposite hand behind her back to stop her from sliding away.

At this point, Winter could feel the orgasm building. Kody continued sucking on her clitoris and fingering her at the same time. She reflexively released the table and grabbed the back of his head. She was close, so close. Then unlike any orgasm she had ever had, her body erupted, bringing waves of pleasure stronger than she thought possible.

Being expectedly sensitive after her delicious orgasm, she begged him to stop. Even made an attempt to get out of his grasp. Either he didn't hear her, or he simply didn't care. Not ready to give her a break, Kody continued teasing, tasting and toying with her.

She was so drained from the release and strong sensations that she laid back onto the table and allowed him to continue having his way with her. He increased the direct pressure on her clitoris with his tongue, and a few minutes later, she came again... and then again.

Finally, he slowly sat back and wiped his mouth.

"Damn, that was good," he said.

She didn't comment. She was too exhausted. She couldn't move, couldn't catch her breath and the world wouldn't stop spinning.

After a moment, he stood. Looked down at her and said, "thanks for the dessert; it was delicious." Then, he picked his jacket, tossed it over his arm and walked out of the door.

◆◆◆

Kody

"Where do you want the tile?" George, one of Kody's employees, asked him the next morning.

"Put it over in the corner," Kody instructed.

George turned and said, "By the way, the cement truck is on the way."

The arrival of the cement truck was wonderful news. When Winter came home today, the broken area in her walkway would be fixed. She had no idea he was going to do it, and he couldn't wait for her to see it. It struck him that she may feel like he was trying to buy her with all the things he did for her. Especially now since he had revealed how much money he had.

That was not his intention at all. He just felt like she was his, and he took care of what was his. There was no reason for her to suffer through or pay for damages to her home if he could fix them. He wanted her safe and stress-free. Basically, he wanted her to be completely happy in and out of the bedroom.

The thought sent him back to last night. Her moans, her taste, her smell. The feeling of her thighs touching his face and her responses to his touch. He loved every minute.

It was kind of funny because, normally, he wasn't big on oral sex. Yeah, he had received it a lot, but he didn't give it often. It wasn't that he had a problem giving; he simply didn't do it much.

Very few women pulled that response out of him, and Winter was certainly one of them. Her whimpers and pleadings for more before her first orgasm, and then to stop once she'd had her first release, fueled his already intense desire for her.

He knew she'd never had an orgasm like that before, and one would have been enough for her, but it wasn't for him.

He couldn't bring himself to stop, so he didn't; instead, he decided to bring her to orgasm twice more. He was almost late to his fucking meeting with Jackson because once he was done tasting her, he wanted to be inside her.

But there was no time. He didn't mind, though; pleasing her was worth it. He wanted her left satisfied, speechless and weak from pleasure, and he'd done that.

He sent up a silent thank you to all the men that had fucked up in her life. If they hadn't, then he wouldn't have her. And have her he did, and he was ready for more.

He walked over and glanced out of his side window that faced her house. He didn't know what he expected to see. She likely had already left for work, and even if she hadn't, she now parked her car in the garage.

Suddenly his phone rang; the display read Winter. He answered and said, "I was just thinking of you."

"Good thoughts, I hope."

"Always. How'd you sleep?

"Really good, thanks to you," she said.

"I'm happy to hear that."

"How's your morning going?" she asked.

"It's good. By the way, I have a surprise for you. You'll see it when you get home today."

He could almost see her smiling through the phone when she said, "Really, what is it?!"

"When you get home," he repeated.

"Fine, you're no fun."

"Hold on a second," he said.

She heard him yell out to someone that he'd be right there. Then into the phone, he said, "Hey, I gotta go."

"Ok. Hey, before you go, was last night always the type of dessert you had planned if you won?

"Yup."

"So actual cakes and pies not even on your radar, huh?"

"Not at all. Bye, gorgeous."

Chapter 16
Winter

Winter spent most of her morning daydreaming about Kody—his face, his body, his touch, his scent, his voice and all those orgasms. He had most definitely left an indelible impression on her. She didn't know anything sexual had the ability to feel that amazing.

Every time she replayed how good it felt having her legs spread wide on that table, she experienced spikes in pressure.

Those soft lips kissing and sucking on her pussy was incredible. She needed to stop thinking about it because she was getting hot and bothered. Hell, merely thinking about him got her hot and bothered.

Why wouldn't it? He was a good man. One unlike any other she had ever known. She had just seen him last night, but she missed him already. She couldn't wait to get home to see him after work. Then she remembered he said he had a surprise for her and wondered what it could be.

He had already done so much; he had to stop this. She didn't want him to feel like she just wanted his money. Although just how much money he had was a recent revelation.

"Millions? Wow," she thought. "That is a lot of money, but it changed nothing. She would have still wanted him if he earned less."

Thinking of money and surprises reminded her that she needed to order his and Mr. Sanders's niece's gifts. She'd concluded they were both getting high-quality, personalized watches. It took some time, but eventually, she found a company she liked and the exact watches she wanted to order.

She first started out her search using the name of the watch Kody was wearing that night at dinner. She wasn't surprised to find it was expensive. It wasn't so much because he seemed materialistic, because he wasn't that way at all, but the watch had a very unique and opulent look to it.

Not to mention, he said his dad collected them, and he was following in those footsteps. Usually, when people collected things, they wanted it to not only stand out and appeal to the eyes, but they liked a certain quality.

However, she had to admit, learning about the difference between a $10 watch from the grocery store and watches that offered more luxury was interesting.

Variables such as labor, materials, and whether it was quartz or mechanical, easily set watches apart and were responsible for sizable price differences.

For Mr. Sanders's niece, she chose a beautiful rose gold watch that displayed time using Roman numerals and showcased a cluster of assorted diamonds. The inscription she picked read:

"I'll always have time for you. Love, Uncle Cordell."

Satisfied with her choice, she ordered the watch. It was immediately followed by a confirmation and a Dec.10th delivery date. She forwarded the order details and confirmation to Mr. Sanders.

For Kody, she'd chosen a black and gold watch with a titanium band, domed sapphire crystal and anti-reflective coating. The inscription on his watch read:

"As long as time is counting, there is no room for doubting."

She thought of the night he told her that his dad always said that to him; he looked so happy and at peace. She always wanted that for him when he thought of his dad.

In her mind, she could already see his handsome face light up when she gave it to him—that heart-melting smile he gave made that much sexier by his soft kissable lips.

She thought, yet again, of those lips and tongue on her less than 24 hours ago, and shivers ran down her spine. She had never felt that type of pleasure and connection with a man, and they hadn't even had sex. If he could do that with his tongue, what could he do with his dick? All she knew was she had to find out.

A knock on her office door caused her to look up. It was Lisa.

"Can I have the completed prop list for the Playground Horror Contract?"

"I'm not done with it. They made a change to some of their prop requests, and I need to modify their contract. I'll be done with it before I head home today, though."

"That works. Have you had lunch yet?"

"No," Winter said, looking down at her stomach as if it could verbally agree.

"I can grab you something from Chipotle or Panera if you want me to. I'm getting something from one of those places but haven't decided which yet."

"I'll take a vegetable soup from Panera, please." She grabbed her wallet out of her purse, pulled out $20, and handed it to Lisa.

"You sure you don't want anything else?" Lisa said, taking the money.

"No, I'm fine, but buy your lunch too; it's on me today."

"Thanks. I'll have to stop by more often when you're hungry," Lisa said and walked away.

Winter finished placing the order for Kody's watch, got the confirmation and jumped back into work. She had two meetings for new filming contracts, and she had to create more prop lists for upcoming films.

Researching the props from various time periods was sometimes consuming because she didn't want to have a car that wasn't made until the 80s be caught in a scene from the 70s.

All in all, she got most of it done by the time she was ready to head home. She had a few projects to finish up on Monday, but their budget was proving to be problematic for the things they would need, so those prop lists may need to be put on hold.

After she got home, she showered, grabbed another pair of her beloved comfortable PJs, and turned on some music. This shirt said, "I sleep better with you" next to it was a woman hugging a glass of wine.

Although the statement on the shirt rang true for her as well, she preferred to abandon the wine and put Kody in its place. His presence had really made a difference in her sleep. She hadn't had a nightmare in weeks now. She hoped they were gone forever.

Kody was there by seven. After giving him a sweet, yummy kiss hello, she asked excitedly, "Where is it?"

He led her out the front door and down her stairs to the walkway.

"Notice anything missing?" he asked.

Her eyes got wide, and she covered her mouth in complete shock. Having a moment to take it all in, she removed her hand and said, "That horrible hump, it's gone! How did you… no, when did you do this?"

She wondered if maybe he did it days ago, and she somehow missed it since she had been entering and exiting the house through the garage.

"I did it early this morning after you left for work. It was an easy fix because the piece that was damaged was already separated from the rest quite a bit. We only had to dig up a little more around it and then lay down the new cement. It blended right in and only took about 45 minutes."

"Is it dry yet?"

"Mostly, but I put markers around it to ensure it not be disturbed before tomorrow."

"I don't know what to say. You are just too kind. Thank you."

He put his arm around her. "Let's go back inside out of this cold, start a fire and we can think of a way for you to repay me."

"I like that idea," she said.

Once they were back inside, and the food was ready, they settled in to eat. It was a nice feeling, enjoying a Friday night, music playing and stress-free.

"You have any weekend plans?" he asked.

"Not much besides hanging out with you. I do have to drop off that nightstand at the women's shelter tomorrow. Sorry I didn't ask you to ride with me to drop it off, but it's for a women's shelter, and you're a man, so… I think you know where I'm going with this."

"No problem. I fully understand. Do you want me to load it into your car for you?"

"I'm good; it's pretty light. Thanks, though."

Done with his food, he got up to take his plate to the sink.

Sitting back down to join her at the table as she took her last bite, he said, "You don't feel like I'm trying to buy you or anything, do you? Money has a way of making things messy, and I never want you to feel like I don't think you are capable of taking care of yourself. It's more so that I am enjoying taking over that role. I love spoiling you and seeing you smile."

"No, I don't think you're trying to buy me, although I need you to stop it with all of the free work for a while. I want you with or without the money. But let's be honest," she said, smiling flirtatiously, "with the money is a lot sexier."

"If it turns you on, all the better," he said.

"Speaking of," she said, looking down at the table and recalling last night. "I still can't believe you did that."

"Why is that?"

" I don't know, but you really caught me off guard."

"That was the point. The question is, did you enjoy it?" he asked.

"I think you can tell from my reaction that I did."

"Yes, but I want to hear you say it."

"Ok then, full disclosure, I fucking loved it. I now understand what all the fuss is about, and I thank you for that."

"It was my pleasure," he said, giving her a wickedly sexy grin.

"What I don't understand is why did you stop? Most men would have moved on to sex, and I was definitely ready for that too."

"Woman, you were barely conscious when I left."

Laughing, she said, "Oh, that. I just needed a quick recharge, and I would have rejoined the party."

"I'll keep that in mind," he said. "Actually, though, I had a meeting with Jackson, I needed to get to. But don't worry, tonight, there are no meetings, and I have all the time in the world."

She felt the familiar throbbing in between her legs, and at the same time, he reached across the table and grabbed her hand.

Smiling, she shook her head. "I just don't get you, Kody. Why are you single? I know you have met someone you could be with by now. You are a man that seems to carry the total package. What gives, does the moving around so much really just make relationships complicated for you?"

Rubbing his thumb lightly over her hand, he said, "The moving around isn't a problem. I simply don't often find what I'm looking for. But you are just as much the total package, so what's your real holdup?" Then pointedly, he added, "And you can't use your taking a break from dating excuse you told me about."

"What can I say? I choose the wrong men, or rather the wrong men choose me. I'm sure your choices with women are a lot better than the choices I have of men to date. I feel like I can't find a good man to save my life."

"Elaborate," he said.

"For instance, a man can probably get several attractive women with a job who are ready to lie down, have his babies and take care of him. While many women get stuck with guys who are too old, have no job, aren't attractive at all, or already have ten kids. Maybe I'm not saying it right; it's kinda hard to explain.

"Goodness, did that come out right? she thought. It made me sound petty or bitter, and I am neither. I just honestly think women have a harder time finding good men than the other way around. But maybe that is just my experiences."

A new song was starting up. It was a love song with a slow and steady rhythm. Kody slowly withdrew his hand from her, folded his arms and stared at her from across the table.

"Try to explain it," he said

Was he getting upset? He didn't look upset, but she wasn't sure—his face was blank.

Searching for the words, she began, "I'm sure you meet plenty of women who want to be with you, but you're probably just too wrapped up in work and stuff. Whereas I wouldn't mind something serious, but I'm barely meeting any potential, you know?"

"No, I don't know, Winter. Do you want to be with me?"

Was he trying to mess with her? She didn't know what to say to that. Of course, she wanted him, but it probably wouldn't work out, plus she wasn't even sure that he wanted to be with her. Finding her escape, she decided to flip the tables on him.

"Do you want me?"

He finally smiled and then said, "I love it when you get flustered. It's cute."

He got up from his chair and walked around to her side of the table. Standing in front of her, he extended his hand. She inserted hers into his, and he pulled her to her feet. Then he drew her close and started dancing.

As she laid her head on his chest, she found herself relaxing. He smelled so good, and his arms around her made her feel at ease. She could stay like this forever, lost to the world and safe in his arms.

After the song ended, her body protested as he pulled away from her. But still holding her hand, he led her to the couch. He sat down and pulled her onto his lap, and for a few minutes, they just sat there watching the fire.

"I want you, and I want to be with you," he said. "But I never want anything from you that you are not ready to give me, that includes your body or your heart."

Staring into the fire, she said, "I want you, too, but isn't this all just a mistake? Won't you be leaving soon?"

"Face me," he said

She repositioned herself on his lap to face him. He looked into her eyes and gently caressed her face with his hands. "I could never leave you."

As if that was the push she needed, she leaned in and began to kiss him. He slowly slid his hands up to run his fingers through her hair, and she moaned softly into his mouth.

Reaching under his shirt, she traced her fingers over his chest, enjoying the smooth, firm muscles under her touch. He broke the kiss for a second and pulled off his shirt.

With her hands back on him and more eager now, she reached down and caressed his hardness. Even through his clothes, she could tell it was long and thick, and she wanted him. She had to have him.

Sliding her fingers into his pants, she could already imagine how good he would feel inside her, then all of a sudden, he grabbed her wrist.

Putting his hand under her chin and lifting her face up to his, he said, "I'm running this show." Then he pulled off her shirt and bra and told her to stand up.

She did as instructed. Once she was completely naked, he sat back on the couch and looked her up and down. Feeling overly exposed with herself being totally naked while he was only missing a shirt, she looked away as if something was suddenly very interesting in the corner of the room.

"Don't do that," he said. "Look at me."

She did. It was a reaction that she didn't even have a chance to think about. He spoke, and her body responded. She understood at that moment that not only did she want to be pleased by him, but she also wanted to please him. To give her body to him any way he wanted.

"Am I making you nervous?" he asked.

Releasing a small laugh and holding her pointer finger and thumb close together, she said, "a little bit."

"Winter, you have to be one of the most beautiful women I have ever seen. Your body is perfect; your mind is perfect. You are perfect." Reaching out, he pulled her to him and gently lifted one of her legs to rest on his shoulder.

She felt his breath moments before his tongue. He was moving it around slowly, and in a teasing manner that felt so good, she found herself grabbing his head to make him speed up the pace.

When he began sucking on her clitoris while rubbing and massaging her lower back, it didn't take long before she could feel the orgasm approaching. She moaned and pulled him closer. But suddenly, he stopped.

Breathing heavily and looking down at him, she said, "Is something wrong?"

"No. I just want to change positions."

Kody slid down to the luxuriously soft rug that stretched the entire width of her couch and pulled Winter down with him.

She was sitting on his stomach. Palms pressed against his chest.

"Slide up," he said.

She complied but only moving forward about an inch. He laughed and said, "How about you keep coming forward until I let you know to stop."

Looking down at his handsome face and chest covered with hard muscles and sex appeal drawing her in, she went for it. She moved up, and once she was up far enough, he guided her over his face, but then her nerves took over, and she stiffened.

Kody could feel the tension in her. He wasn't surprised. He got the feeling that she had never tried this before. Sex for her was probably typical and not very eventful. Well, he was about to change that.

"Winter, I'm not going to break. Just relax."

Pulling her down onto his mouth, he easily found the exact spot that not only gave her pleasure but reflexively caused her body to relax.

As Kody continued swirling his tongue, sucking and licking, she felt the explosion creeping up once again. She positioned her hands above his head and leaned forward.

Without realizing it, she started grinding on his face. The loss of control must have been exactly what Kody wanted because he tightened his grip around her waist, and she heard him moan with pleasure.

Her release was soon to follow. It left her shaking and calling his name. Once her breathing calmed, he lifted her off him and repositioned them so that she was lying down, and he was on top of her.

He began kissing all over her body—her legs, her waist, her stomach. When he made it to her breast, he gently bit and sucked on her nipples.

As the the pulsating inside her seemed to start again, she pulled him to her, and their lips met. Tasting herself on his tongue somehow turned her on more.

"You aren't going to dine and run like you did last time, are you?" she asked.

"Not a chance," he said between kisses.

He continued teasing and touching her for what seemed like forever. He was driving her out of her mind. Moving his tongue and lips over her jawline, neck, breast, stomach, thighs, it all felt so good and pissed her off so bad at the same time.

Her ache for him was maddening. She wanted him more than she had wanted any man. When she would try to pull him closer, he would back up just slightly, making it very clear that this ride was his to control.

After what seemed like endless torture, she felt him enter her. He moved slowly at first as if making sure she felt every inch of him.

"When did? How did?"

She was confused, and her thoughts weren't forming completely. She was trying to understand when he removed his pants. She was in such a zone, and her body was so ignited that she couldn't recall a moment where he hadn't been touching her.

But at this point, it didn't matter, and she didn't care.

The heightened pleasure of stretching and fullness took over as he moved inside her and satisfied her in ways that she didn't even know she craved.

Wrapping her legs around his waist, he slid deeper and increased the pace. Their bodies moved in a rhythm that seemed to naturally complement each other. It took no effort, no thinking, just being. She couldn't stop moaning as he thrust into her time after sweet time.

He accompanied the physical stimulation with some mental by telling her how beautiful she was and how much he wanted her.

Nothing, Winter thought, should ever feel this good. She felt another orgasm approaching, different from the first because this one was from him being inside her.

It was somehow stronger and made her feel as if she was coming apart. Without restraint the euphoric waves of the orgasm consumed her, and her body shook and tingled with warm satisfaction.

He pinned her arms down above her head, and her body seemed to melt into the smooth plush rug that laid beneath them.

Kody continued to thrust into her, making his intentions understood that the night was far from over. She bit her lip as her body surrendered to him, and she tried to keep up with his demands.

The pleasure zones he was hitting inside her; she didn't even know existed. It was as if he was internally massaging the stress and buildup of years of sexual frustration away.

Every so often, he would turn her in another position, and she'd feel the intensity of another climax building from deep within.

When he finally switched her from her side onto her back for the third time, she had to tap out. Between the mind-numbing ecstasy and sheer exhaustion, she was too limp to do more.

Finally, when another orgasm broke free, Kody came with her, and her already useless legs began to shake so much they no longer felt connected to her body.

Afterward, they laid there in silence, listening to the fire pop and crackle. She laid on his chest, satisfied, and completely spent.

He had literally fucked her senseless, just like she thought he would. She couldn't think; she couldn't move; she couldn't breathe. She couldn't even see. Well, the last one was likely because her eyes were closed, but she wouldn't put it past him.

This man was everything. She could feel herself falling asleep moments before she actually did. Her last coherent thought was that she wasn't falling for Kody. She had already fallen.

Chapter 17
Winter

The next morning she woke up, and Kody was gone. Her paranoia of him being no longer interested because he'd finally gotten what he wanted all along started to creep in. But she shut it down, reminding herself that Kody was a good man who cared about her.

A clanging noise in the kitchen made her bolt straight up. Kody was there, in the kitchen, cooking breakfast. She smiled at him.

"I'm sorry, did I wake you?"

"No, you didn't," she said.

Getting up on her feet, she took a moment to stretch and then walked to the bathroom to freshen herself up.

Returning to the kitchen, she walked over to him and put her arms around his waist. Taking the pan for the eggs off the stove, he turned to look at her.

"Hey, sexy," she said.

"Hey, gorgeous," he responded.

He picked her up, and she wrapped her legs around him. Kissing him deeply, as he held her close, she couldn't think of another place she'd rather be. He put her down and got back to setting up breakfast while she went to have a seat at the table.

"Were you trying to kill me last night?" she said.

"Nope, you just got what you deserved."

"Kody! Are you still mad about my not being able to please a woman comment? You got me back for that, remember? You basically left me unconscious right here on this very table?"

"I remember, doesn't mean I was done with making you pay for it."

She smiled and rolled her eyes. "Well, thank you for making me eat those words."

"Anytime."

"How long have you been up?" she asked.

"A couple of hours."

"Wow. I didn't hear you moving around."

"Yeah, you were sleeping pretty soundly, but I tried my best to be quiet while I showered, had some coffee and even answered a few emails all before making you breakfast."

"I slept through all that? What in the hell did you do to me?"

Putting her food down on the table, then sitting across from her, he said, "nothing I don't plan on doing again."

"I certainly hope so," she said. "Wait, where's your breakfast?"

"I'm not hungry. I don't normally eat breakfast. A cup of coffee and I'm good. But you enjoy. Besides, I need to get ready to go soon. One of my guys won't be able to pick up the things I'll need on Monday, so I'm going to head to the warehouse and pick it up."

"How long will that take?"

"Only a few hours. Will you be here?" he asked.

"Not sure. I'm going to head to the shelter once I'm done with breakfast. Then I have a few more errands and some things to pick up for work. That reminds me, would you like to come by the office and have lunch with me sometime next week?"

"That would be nice. Is any day fine with you?"

"Yes."

"Ok, I'll let you know then."

He stood to leave and then leaned close to her ear. "Make sure you eat up; you're going to need your energy." Then he kissed her again and left.

Instantly she missed him. Wanted more of his touch, his presence and to enjoy any and everything he had to offer. She looked down at the delicious food and said, "guess I'll have to enjoy this instead," and dug in.

◆◆◆

"Winter! Did you bring us another one of your fancy pieces?" Mrs. Gordon asked.

Mrs. Gordon was a sweet old lady in her 70's, who had been running Heart and Home, the local Women's shelter, for over fifteen years. She always got excited when Winter stopped by and always welcomed her redesigned antiques.

"I wouldn't call them fancy, but yes, I brought a nightstand." Winter stepped aside so that Mrs. Gordon could look at the piece.

"Oh, don't be modest. It is exquisite. Did you paint this one too and add those little, shiny stones?"

"Yes, I did."

"Great job! And I know who it would be perfect for. One of the ladies just got approved for a house and has a 12-year-old daughter, and another on the way, bless her heart. I think this would go perfect in the daughter's room."

Winter beamed. "Oh, wow, that's wonderful. I am so glad I could help."

"You always do, sweetie. Tell me, how have you been? Any boyfriends or maybe babies on the way?"

Mrs. Gordon made the statement while lightly laying a hand on Winter's stomach. Mrs. Gordon loved children. A lot of the people at the shelter referred to her as Mama Gordon. She was very kind and did anything she could if the outcome would benefit the kids.

Smiling happily, Winter said, "there is a man, but no baby."

"Well, dear, at least we have the first base covered. Don't worry, children will come soon enough."

Winter laughed and then abruptly stopped. The comment on kids made her mentally dive back into her night of passion.

"Did he use a condom? Of course, he did, right? Or maybe he didn't? She was so wrapped up in the

moment, she didn't even think. Idiot!!" she mentally yelled at herself.

"You alright? You looked startled," Mrs. Gordon asked.

"I'm fine. I just realized I may have left the stove on, " she lied. It was the first thing she could think of.

"I'm sorry, Mrs. Gordon, I have to go. Is everything fine with the nightstand? Can I leave it here, or do you need me to carry it into your office?"

"No, No, here is fine. You go check on that stove. Wouldn't want you losing your place and having to move in with us."

Winter rushed for the door and ran to her car.

She kept replaying the night, trying to locate at least one detail that would jog her memory and guarantee her he used protection. But how could she remember him putting on a condom when she didn't even remember him pulling off his pants. His fucking pants! She had been reckless.

"Think, Winter, think. Yes, you don't remember him pulling off his pants, but it did happen; you know that for a fact. Same truth could apply to the condom."

It was wishful thinking, but she needed something to cling to. She blew out a breath and glanced at her cell in the passenger seat. This was nothing to ask him over the phone.

She needed to keep her cool and wait until she saw him in a few hours. For now, she should just finish up her errands and ask him later. Prematurely freaking out will benefit no one. Trying her best to drown out her worrying thoughts, she turned on some music and proceeded with her day in an attempt to avoid falling apart.

About four hours later, she was home and still in one piece. Kody had sent her a text about an hour ago, and she told him she'd text him once she got in. She pulled in the garage and went over the details again, drawing a blank. She knew what that meant.

She would have to ask him if he used a condom. In her mind, asking him that made her sound so irresponsible and stupid.

What if he said no? Then she could possibly have a little Kody in the next nine months, that's what. She paused as the possibility of a child with Kody danced in her mind.

Envisioning him holding a precious bundle and all the things they could do as a family made the idea not as scary as it originally seemed. It would actually be nice to have a child with a man so warm, kind, strong and levelheaded.

"BUT NOT RIGHT NOW!" the logical part of her brain screamed at her.

It was true, as nice as the idea of that might be, she was not ready for that… they were not ready for that. She still didn't even know how they were going to work their relationship out. He said he could never leave her, but what did that mean? Was he simply not going back to California? He couldn't do that.

Getting out of the car, she began unloading the groceries and various other household items from the trunk. When she was done, she put everything away and started a load of laundry.

Picking up her phone, she texted Kody that he could come over whenever he was ready. He sent an instant reply that he'd be over soon.

To keep her mind occupied, she opened her laptop and decided to work on more prop lists for clients. Kody was there an hour later on the couch watching some car show she was unfamiliar with.

"Would you ever like to go and see a hockey game?" he asked without looking away from the TV.

"Yeah, I hear those games can be highly entertaining with the fights between teams."

"That's actually true. I haven't been to a hockey game since I was a kid, but I remember I loved it."

The mention of being a kid gave her the push she needed to ask him about last night.

"Listen, last night was…amazing, for lack of a better word."

"I agree," he said, still watching TV.

"I can't believe I have to ask this. I'm so embarrassed. It's not like me to be so careless. But did you use protection?"

He picked up the remote, turned off the TV then turned to face her. "Yes."

She felt like a weight had been lifted off her shoulders. But somewhere far in the distance, there was a tiny twinge of sadness as the confirmation of no little Kody, at least not yet, in their future.

"Seriously? I don't even remember you putting it on?"

"You also don't remember me getting completely undressed," he said with the lift of a brow.

Confused, she asked. "How did you know that?"

"Because I pay attention. Your surprise was evident as soon as I entered you. You were in your own little world."

She smiled at him. "Yeah, that was some world I'd like to revisit it really soon."

"I'm ready if you are," he said.

She wanted to go over there and jump on him at that very moment, but she had another topic on her mind.

"There's something else," she said. "Last night, when you mentioned you could never leave me, what did you mean? Are you moving here?

"Eventually, yes, but not right away. I have a few more projects in California and Texas that I would like to complete first. I'll have to work out the details, but I will stop getting involved with new contracts in California and Texas and get more involved with projects here. Also, I'd only travel maybe five months out of the year and not nine or ten."

"Travel? You mean that you might be gone five months at a time?"

"Sometimes?"

"Oh, ok, " she said. She felt her fear spike. What he was explaining sounded a lot like a long-distance relationship. She didn't want that. Long-distance relationships were not ideal, not for her anyway. People always fell apart, she knew from experience.

At the same time, she didn't want to say that to him. His company was important to him, as it should be. He had worked hard to get where he was, and she felt she had no right to push the issue. He was already making major adjustments for her. Five months out of the year wasn't bad; just because her other relationship failed didn't mean theirs would, right?

"Winter?"

"Yes," she said, adding a smile that didn't quite reach her eyes.

"Come sit with me."

She came to sit on the couch next to him.

Grabbing her hands, he said, "I can see that brain of yours churning away. It's going to be ok. What we have is real; it won't fade just because we will be apart sometimes. I know you told me that you had a failed long-distance relationship in the past, but this is not that relationship. Plus, you can even come to see me when I do the projects anytime you'd like."

Feeling better due to Kody putting her fears at ease, she said, "visiting you while working is fine, but staying in one of the renovations is not? I love you, but no thank you."

She closed her mouth and tried to stand up. She could not believe she had just said that. Yes, it was true, she did love him, but she still didn't want him to know it. What if he thought she was crazy? She had to leave the room. She had to get away. But he wouldn't let her hand go.

"Look at me," he said.

It took effort, but she eventually did.

"I love you too, Winter. I think I have loved you for a while now, but I didn't want to say anything and scare you back into your shell. You may have thought I was lying if I said it too fast, but I promise you, I do love you."

She stared into his eyes. He was telling the truth. She couldn't be more happy, more excited, more touched, more… turned on. Just when she thought love may not have been in the cards for her, she lands a full deck with this gorgeous, wonderful, patient, bold man.

She needed him, his lips on hers and his hands caressing her body. She grabbed his shirt and pulled him to her. A repeat of last night would be the perfect way to end the evening.

◆◆◆

"There is a fine ass man here to see you," Lisa said, standing in Winters office doorway, fanning herself.

"That's Kody. You can send him back."

"Oh, that explains it."

"Explains what?" Winter asked, confused.

"Why you've been so happy?"

"I'm always happy."

"True. But you've been especially happy lately. It's a type of happy that only love and a man tapping that ass can produce."

"Is it that obvious?"

"Yup. It's all over your vibe, and I'm happy for you. He's a good one, Winter."

"How do you know?"

"I just do," she said confidently. "I'll send him back."

Chapter 18
Kody

"The house looks amazing," Winter said as she slowly walked around the small ranch style home that no longer bore even the slightest resemblance to her own.

Kody watched her as she admired the newly installed skylight and detailed tile design in the kitchen area. She was wearing blue jeans, heels and a pink and yellow sweater that hugged her breasts. Her hair was down, and she looked so damn good.

All he could think about was grabbing a hand full of those beautiful black curls and fucking her as she was bent over the counter. He could feel his hardness starting as the scene played out in his mind. Later he would definitely tend to those needs.

"You have done a whole lot in four months. I'm so proud of you," she said.

The comment made him laugh.

She turned to face him. "What's so funny?"

"Saying that you are proud of me. It's sweet, but that's something I don't hear often. I think the last person that told me that was my grandma about two years ago."

"Well, you should hear it more often. You do great work."

"Thanks, babe. I'll let Jackson know he needs to do a better job cheering me on."

"Maybe he'd agree," she said jokingly.

"What he'd do is call me a pussy and hang up on me, and I'd have to agree with him."

"You guys are silly," she said, heading towards the master bedroom. He knew the exact moment she saw the master bath because she let out a sequel of delight.

"KODY, I LOVE THIS BATHROOM!"

"I figured you would," he said, joining her in the newly designed en suite. "If you'd like, I can design you something similar."

"Don't play with me," she said, pushing his arm. "I'd never leave the shower. You'd seriously do this for me?"

He wasn't surprised by her question. Although he'd made it known several times that he would do anything in his power for her, she just wasn't that type of person.

She never expected him to give her anything beyond the normal expectations, of course, but it was for that very reason that he wanted to give her everything.

"Winter, have I not proved to you that I would do anything for you?"

"I know," she said, looking around the bathroom. "It's just so nice! I love how you added the standalone tub with the faucet coming out of the floor. Then the shower has built-in bench seats on each side, with an area to seat a chair by the window. It's like a spa in here."

"And your design would be even better," he said, kissing her on the forehead.

She finished touring the house, and he told her what details he had left to complete. There wasn't much. He just needed to finish up painting throughout the house, replacing doors, new flooring and things of that caliber.

Outside, he planned on building a covering for the oversized deck they had completed. With nothing more to see, they decided to watch a movie and relax in front of the fireplace at Winter's house.

Stepping out onto the porch, Kody noticed a box in the corner that he hadn't seen earlier. Retrieving it, he saw that it was addressed to Winter Daniels.

"Looks like the mail people are at it again," he said, handing her the box.

Confusion turned to understanding as she took the box and said. "Well, at least this time they got it half right."

"What do you mean?"

"This box contains something for you, even though they were supposed to deliver it to me."

"Well, aren't you going to give it to me then?"

"Later," she said, tucking the box under her arm and heading next door.

Once they got settled, Winter grabbed two glasses, a bottle of wine and joined him on the couch. After pouring them both a glass, she searched for a movie to watch.

Flipping through the channels and displaying her lack of enthusiasm with the choices, she finally stopped when she got to a movie showing a pizza guy standing inside the entryway of a house, trying to get any of the many people in the house to help him collect payment.

"I love Home Alone. Are you fine watching this?" she said.

"Works for me."

They watched the movie and sipped their wine, laughing and commenting at all the appropriate scenes. As the movie came to an end, he slid his hand under her sweater and began rubbing his fingers up and down her sides. He could tell she was getting turned on and about to let him have his fun, then she sat up and pulled away.

"In a second, I have something for you first."

Tearing herself away from him, she grabbed the box that had been left on his porch by accident. Returning to the couch, she presented it to him, and he opened it.

It was a watch. But not just any watch. A stylish, highly likely handmade, Swiss luxury watch. It fit his exact style and taste. Turning it over, he saw the inscription.

"As long as time is counting, there is no room for doubting."

Words of encouragement from his dad. He was so astonished by her thoughtfulness, he was almost speechless. This had to have been the best gift anyone had ever given him.

"Winter," he said, looking at the watch and then up at her. "I can't believe you did this."

"Of course, I did. I love you, and you deserve it."

"This couldn't have been cheap."

Laughing, she said, "it wasn't, but it's fine. It's not like it cost anywhere near the watch you were wearing the night you told me about your watch collection."

He just looked at her for a moment while smiling and shaking his head. "I don't know what to say. I love you and thank you so much; this is very kind of you."

"You are more than welcome."

"How did I get so lucky?" he said, touching her and thinking of all the things he wanted to do to her.

"Oh, you haven't gotten lucky yet. But you're about to," she said, biting her lip. She knew what that did to him. He pulled her in for a kiss. Pulling away before he had his fill of her succulent lips, she took the watch and box from his lap and set it on the coffee table.

Moving down to get on the floor in front of him and undoing his jeans. she said, "I want you to just sit back and relax while I handle the show this evening."

Not one to argue, he sat back and did what he was told.

◆◆◆

The next month and a half arrived quicker than Kody wanted or expected. It was early February, and he and Winter were heading to Jackson and Erica's place for a Super Bowl party. They were getting there before the crowd so that Winter could spend time with Erica while he with Jackson.

The day had started off perfectly. After having sex three times, they finally but grudgingly got out of bed and got ready for the day. A quick breakfast for Winter and a cup of coffee for Kody, then they made their way to the store to get some items for the party. Jackson and Erica insisted they didn't need to bring anything, but neither felt comfortable showing up empty-handed.

Damn, he loved her. Placing his hand over hers as they drew closer to his cousin's house, it was apparent to him that he needed to reconsider his work structure. He told Winter that his plan was to return to California and Texas to oversee a few projects that were coming to an end.

Then moving forward, he would decrease his workload in those states and increase his involvement in the Georgia work assignments. But now, he was rethinking the whole thing.

He was no longer sure that he was fine being away from her that long. He wanted to wake up to her every morning and fall asleep with her every night.

As far as his house in California went, listing it and renting one in Georgia would be no big deal. As things pertained to work, he could easily appoint someone else to oversee the projects and travel only when needed, just like Jackson did.

However, he had been working wherever he was needed for so long it was hard to let it go. He was used to seeing specific projects through to the end and ensuring that his employees exceeded expectations. Old habits did die hard, after all.

It would be an unquestionable adjustment to let someone else handle that, but he had very capable management. That was why he and Jackson chose the people they did. It was time for a change, and even though it was an unfamiliar one, he was ready.

Pulling up at Jackson's house and grabbing things out of the truck. He heard Jackson coming before he saw him.

"Didn't I tell you guys not to bring anything?"

"You did, but no one listens to you," Kody responded.

Jackson walked towards Kody with his arms open as if to help grab some of the groceries. At the last second, when Kody offered him a case of beer to carry, Jackson swerved around him and instead hugged Winter.

"Winter, it's so good to see you."

"You too, Jackson."

"Erica is waiting for you in the house. She's ready to give you a tour and start her chronicles of girl talk."

Winter laughed. "Kody, do you want me to take something in?"

"No, babe, I got it."

"He has it," Jackson said at the same time.

She shook her head and went inside to join Erica.

"Little cousin," Jackson said, turning to Kody. "Are you ready to kick back, let loose and watch what better be one fucking amazing game?"

"I think I'm past ready. Been working tons lately finishing up the house, and we've barely seen each other, man."

"It's because Winter has you wanting to spend all your free time with her."

"She does, and I wouldn't change it. Not to mention, I can see you anytime when I move here."

Jackson stepped back. "Are you kidding me? You're going to relocate to Georgia?"

"Yup." Then in a hushed tone, he said, "Don't say anything to Winter; I have some things to settle in Texas and California before I tell her."

"Well, damn," Jackson said, pulling his cousin in for a hug. "My lips are sealed, and the timing is perfect because we have a contract coming up in Rome, Georgia. It's about an hour and forty-five minutes from here. I am going to need you to go down there and take a meeting in the next week or so."

"Sounds good to me."

"Damn, little cousin, I missed you," Jackson said, then he picked up two cases of beer, and they went inside.

The Super Bowl party was festive and entertaining. Erica had decorated the living room and deck with bold colors and signs from her favorite team.

She had streamers hanging from various areas throughout the living room, a green rug underneath the food table designed like the football field, team-inspired plates and napkins, football-shaped serving dishes and even referee koozies for the beer.

Their house was huge, so Kody assumed it either took her a long time to do this herself, or she poured all the work on Jackson. It was likely the latter. Erica always got Jackson to do her dirty work because he loved her so much.

But it was hard not to; Erica was kind, funny and like a sister to him. Both she and Jackson were always looking out for him and calling to check on him.

When he did finally tell her that he would relocate to Georgia, that is, if Jackson didn't spill the beans first, she would be so excited. She wanted him to be settled and find someone just as bad, if not more than Jackson did.

Lucky for her, he had found someone. Winter was the woman for him. Staring at her across the room with Erica as they chatted in hushed, hushed tones, his heart warmed. He was in the house with the three people that meant the world to him.

As time moved along, more people started to arrive. By the time kick-off happened, there were more than fifty screaming, excited football fans present.

Kody knew a few of them, but not many. With all the moving around he did, it was hard for him to get to know people the way Jackson had. There were a few good friends back in California, but for the most part, everyone else was just associates.

Winter was definitely enjoying herself as she drank beers and shouted at the screen with the rest of them. Kody spent most of the first half of the game cheering and chatting with everyone around.

As half time approached, he decided to grab his beer and spend some time by the patio door. Jackson was grilling, and the cool breeze flowing in every time he opened the door felt nice. With so many people around and the fireplace going, it was starting to get very warm inside.

"Need any help?" Kody asked as Jackson balanced a tray full of hotdogs and grilled wings.

"Normally, I'd say yes, but today you're my guest so just enjoy the game. Plus, your girl is on the way over," Jackson said, nodding in the direction of an approaching Winter.

This was now her third time coming over to "check on him." He knew what she was really doing. She was trying to start trouble.

Each time she came over previously, she would rub her breasts against him or caress his chest or arms seductively. Then she would bite her lip and say, "Oh, excuse me," with a mischievous little grin on her face.

In response to her teasing, he had said nothing. Opting instead to just lock eyes with her and continue to sip his beer. Then as she walked away, he admired just how enticing her ass looked in those jeans.

He knew she was trying to get a rise out of him, but he wasn't going to give in, not yet anyway. He wanted to see what she would do next.

At this moment, she was approaching him yet again, as the half time show was about to start. She discreetly slid her hands down his chest and grabbed his dick.

Then once again, she turned to walk away, but this time he grabbed her arm, and with her back to him, he leaned down and whispered in her ear, "if you keep playing with me, I'm going to take you upstairs and fuck the shit out of you and make sure everyone at this party can hear you screaming my name. So unless you want to be the star of this year's half time show, I suggest you stop toying with me."

He heard her suck in a depth breath, and he laughed. She didn't tease him anymore after that, and he figured she wouldn't. He wasn't bluffing, and he knew Winter knew it. She was sexually adventurous but only to a point. Sure, she could risk having sex in the truck on a deserted road, but at his cousin's house, where Jackson or Erica could hear, she would be mortified.

But even though she had waved the white flag and stopped her touches that did things to him like no other woman ever had, he wasn't letting her off the hook. When they got home, she was his.

Chapter 19
Winter

"Say it," he said.

She wasn't going to. True, what he was doing to her body should be illegal. It felt so amazing, but he couldn't get her to say anything, even if he did possess the best bedroom skills she had experienced.

"No," she tried to say convincingly, but it left her lips in a breathless whimper instead.

"I can keep this up all day," he said into her ear.

"Ugh!" She knew he could. Maybe he'd stop for a break here and there, but his sexual appetite should have been studied. And she wanted to say it, she wanted to so bad, but then he'd win, so no way.

Then as if he knew she still had an ounce of control left, he switched his angle and hit a spot that made the flood gates open. She honestly thought she was going to pass out from the sensation.

She surrendered then, her body brimming with yet another orgasm. "I love you, Kody."

Kissing her neck and then moving up to her lips, he said, "I love you too."

She was exhausted, and worse, she'd lost, which meant she'd have to cook dinner for a week. She didn't mind the punishment; she still cooked for him a lot, that is, when he wasn't cooking for her. She just didn't want to lose.

It had started out as a joke when he asked her if she'd make him her Indian dish he loved.

"Why would I do that?" she asked him playfully.

"Because you love me."

"Hmmm, I'm not sure. I think I just say that sometimes to get my way," she said.

"Oh, do you now? Well, I'll bet I can make you say it again. And if I can, how about you cook me dinner for a week?"

"I accept your challenge, and I won't be saying anything."

He pulled her in for a kiss, which led to more kissing and then eventually sex. She was strong and put up a good fight, but she was no match in the end.

Lying there, basking in the afterglow, she said, "Ashley was right."

"Excuse me,".

"The night I ran into Ashley, she told me that you are a beast in bed."

He laughed to himself. "Well, I do love sex."

"Yes, you do," she said, running her fingers over his chest. "Which also still surprises me that you didn't push for sex any sooner. You have a big appetite, how'd you suppress that?

"You do realize I'm an adult, right? I control sex, not the other way around. But most importantly, no matter how bad I wanted to make you cry out my name, you needed time, and things worked out better because you made the decision when you were comfortable."

"You're so sweet, Kody."

His phone rang. He glanced at the display and then quickly got up.

"I'll be right back," he said.

She thought it odd that he left the room. He never did when he took calls. But the thought was fleeting and not worth pondering over. Instead, lying on her stomach with her legs bent up in the air, she thought about what he said concerning opening up on her own terms. It was true.

Even though it was only a few months, it was the time she needed to feel comfortable and accept that fail or succeed, she wanted to try at a relationship with Kody. She still didn't love the idea that he would be gone, possibly up to five months out of the year, but everything would work out. They genuinely loved each other, and that alone gave them a better chance at surviving than any other relationship she'd had.

Kody came back into the room and got into bed. He laid back on the pillow and placed his phone on the nightstand.

"Everything ok?" she asked.

"Yup," he said, not being any more forthcoming. "You want to go out for lunch?"

"I'd like that."

Then with her mood seeming to dip, she said, "I hate that you are leaving tomorrow. I'm going to miss you."

"I'll miss you too, but I'll be back Wednesday, that's only a few days. Also, cheer up, I have a surprise for you."

"Kody, I told you, no more surprises! At least not right now."

"I never agreed to that. Either way, you'll want this surprise. In addition to lunch, how about we go antique shopping?"

She put her hand to her heart. "Seriously, you'd go antique shopping with me? You know that is my favorite thing in the world?"

"Besides me, I hope."

"That goes without saying. Wait, guys don't volunteer for shopping. What are you trying to get out of me, mister?"

"More orgasms would be good," he said.

Winter laughed.

"The last guy I dated avoided antique shopping like the plague. After a while, it was really entertaining hearing the excuses he would come up with to avoid going. He sprained his ankles."

"As in both?" Kody asked.

"Yup. Then there was the excuse that his long lost cousin showed up on his doorstep. And the one about the neighbor's dog got lost, and he had to organize the search party."

Kody laughed out loud at the last one. "Are you kidding?"

"Sadly, I'm not. He was a real piece of work."

"I don't know, maybe he had the right idea. If antique shopping is really that bad, I guess I better collect my payment before we leave."

"Huh?" Winter said, not following.

"I already told you. I want more orgasms out of you."

Then he instructed her to roll over to her back. He placed one hand between her legs and slide his fingers over her wetness. "So pay up."

◆◆◆

Work on Monday was busy but productive. Winter was able to complete all of her lists for scene setups for the rest of the month.

She was happy to keep her mind busy because even though he'd just left that morning, she missed Kody already.

Not cuddling with him at night would feel odd. Funny how, in such a short amount of time, things seemed like they had been that way forever. As if *they* had always been.

His absence brought to the forefront the question of when he would be returning back to California. He still had a month left on the renovation property, but would he leave soon after?

The last they spoke about it, he told her that he would start shifting his focus to doing more work in Georgia and spending no more than five months out of the year away.

She wondered if anything had changed and when the five months would start.

When he returned from the trip, she would ask him if he'd made any progress in sorting out the details. A knock at the door grabbed her attention.

"Guess what?" Lisa said with a huge smile, entering her office and lowering herself into a chair.

"What?"

"The clients you were supposed to meet with at 1 canceled for today. They rescheduled it for next week."

"Ok, but what's with the excitement? Meeting with them was no big deal; I'm actually ahead in my work for a change, so there were no timing issues."

"Yeah, yeah, but now that means you can have a long lunch with yours truly. It's been forever since we were able to go to lunch together."

"It would be nice to catch up. And you know what?" Winter said, really liking the idea, "we can go to that burger place we went to earlier this year."

"I'll grab my purse and meet you in the parking lot in five minutes," Lisa said as she jumped up to leave.

◆◆◆

They chose a booth table at Tilted Tavern. The place was well known for their delicious hamburgers and fun Karaoke entertainment. Winter, Jessica, Lisa and Chloe had met up there after work several times and sang their joys and sorrows out on that stage more times than they liked to remember.

After placing their orders with the waitress, Lisa leaned in.

"Ok, share."

"Well, his name is Kody," Winter began, "and he is amazing…" She told Lisa the story of how they met, met again and then came to be how they were today, in love and happy.

When winter was done, Lisa said, "Wow. Now that is something they should make a film about. Such a cute love story. Women everywhere would be hanging out in dim lit parking lots, in hopes of getting attacked just so that a mouthwatering, sexy, Godsend like Kody could come and save them."

"I have to admit, I agree. Well, except for the part about women hanging out in parking lots waiting to be rescued, I hope no one would do that."

Shrugging, Lisa said, "crazier things have happened. You know how people get when they see movies they love; they want it to play out in their own lives, so sometimes they try to set the ball in motion. Like how the movie "Fight Club" made people start real fight clubs."

"True," Winter said, nodding.

"Anyway, lonely woman drama aside, I am so happy for you. I could tell when I met Kody that he was a great guy. It's been a long time since you dated anyone. It's good you let your wall down and let someone in."

"Yeah. Kody does work construction, so it was kinda like he demolished my wall without my permission, I might add. But I'm glad he did it."

"See," Lisa said, putting her hand to her chest. "So romantic. I need to find someone that makes me feel like that. Maybe I should take my own advice and wait in one of those dark alleys."

"Stop it. You met tons of men, and I know the one for you is coming along soon."

"You might be right. I did just meet this guy named Paul. Who knows, it could work out. My parents want to set me up with some nice Asian guy, but I like to find my own men, and Paul ain't Asian."

"You know, parents always want what's best for us, according to them anyway."

"Exactly," Lisa said. "Hey, how's Jessica and Chloe."

"They are really good. I talked to them both last week. Chloe is preparing to go to the Dominican Republic for work, and Jessica is super busy planning an event for some wealthy wine company owner."

"I love their lives," Lisa said.

"Hey now," Winter scoffed. "You and I didn't do so bad ourselves. Working in film is fun."

"I guess you're right. It may not be on the beach, but we can always put up a beach backdrop."

"Cheers to that," Winter said, raising her cup of water and taking a sip.

◆◆◆

With work done for the day, Winter found herself sitting in a house that somehow seemed emptier.

She made a chicken sandwich for dinner and exchanged texts with Jessica.

A couple of hours later, she was in bed, flipping through channels when her cell rang. She saw it was Kody and immediately smiled to herself.

"Hey, handsome," she said, answering the call.

"Hey, sweetie. How are you?"

"I'm good. And you? Are things looking promising for the new contract?"

"Yeah, I think the community is going to look great. They have 30 acres cleared out and want to build 25, nicely-sized, single-family homes on it. What are you doing?"

"Lying in bed, flipping through channels. You back at your hotel?"

"Yes, I am. I'm in bed staring up at the ceiling."

"Hmm, are you naked and touching yourself?" she asked.

"No, and I'm not going to, but I want you to."

She laughed.

"I'm serious," he said.

She rolled over onto her stomach. "Why exactly would I do that?"

"Because I want you to cum."

She sat up. She'd never done the whole phone sex thing before. Could be interesting. "You're serious?"

"I'd prefer you say, yes, Kody, I'd love to."

She glanced over at her nightstand drawer that held her pink pulsating vibrator and grinned.

"I think I can do that. One sec." She grabbed her vibrator out of the drawer and then sat back on the bed. "Got my toy, I'm ready."

"Take off your shorts and underwear and then lie back. Open your legs nice and wide and close your eyes."

She did as instructed.

"Turn on your vibrator and start massaging your pussy with it. While you're doing it, I want you to think back to the first time I went down on you at your kitchen table. Are you with me, Winter?"

"Yes," she said, licking her lips and feeling her temperature rising.

"Do you know when I got home I could not stop thinking about how good you tasted?"

"No. I didn't know that," she said, moving the vibrator in a slow up and down motion.

"Oh, yes. Your sweet taste lingered on my lips and tongue as I kept replaying hearing you moan and call out my name. After your first orgasm, I couldn't stop; it was so good, I needed more, so I kept going. Honestly, I could have done that to you for hours. I hate I had to stop when I did."

Her breathing started to increase, and she began closing her legs some.

As if he could see her, he said. "Keep your legs open; you're more sensitive that way, and you'll get wetter."

Opening her legs again, she moved her free hand up to her breast.

"I wish I was there to taste you right now and then slide into you and hit that spot I know you love."

Her body jerked as it reacted to the sheer memory of the feeling she got whenever he pushed inside her. Squeezing her nipples, she was getting close and loving it.

For almost 30 seconds, he said nothing. There was complete silence on the other end. But she was so lost in the incredible sensations coursing through her body that she barely noticed.

Then finally, in a low voice, she heard him say, "Winter."

"Yes," she said, barely audible.

"Turn off your vibrator."

"Huh? What do you.."

"Off," he said sternly.

She swallowed and did what he said. "But... but," she said, breathing heavily. "I thought you wanted me to cum."

"I do, when I'm there and inside you and not a second before. Until then, I want you turned on and ready for me. Tomorrow night, I'll call you, and I want you to do the exact same thing. When I get home Wednesday, I will take care of the rest. Understand?"

"Yes," she said with an evident pouting in her voice.

"Good. Now, get some sleep. I love you."

"Love you too," she said, feeling hot and oh so terribly bothered.

The next morning, she woke up close to 8 a.m. Since she had gotten so much accomplished at work yesterday, she decided she'd go in to the office closer to 9:30.

She started her pot of coffee and went in search of something to wear for the day. With it being fairly cold outside, she settled on some tan business slacks with a blue and silver sweater.

Walking back to the kitchen, she saw the lamps that she'd found while antique shopping with Kody the other day. The rest of the stuff she found, a table and a really cool circular mirror, was out in the garage.

She didn't know what changes she would make to the mirror yet, but she was sure she would think of something. The lamps didn't need much of anything but to be re-polished. They would look nice in her guest bedroom on either side of the bed. Once they were clean, they would go to their new home.

The thought made her miss her mom. They used to go antique shopping together. She wondered what ideas her mom would have for the table she just got.

Maybe later she could look through some old photo albums of work her mom did and draw some inspiration. For now, she would work on quelling her hunger and make a cheese toast to go with her coffee.

She ate her breakfast while looking over work emails. Nothing new or of top priority had come in, which meant she could help out setting up scenes instead of performing her normal desk job duties.

By 9:26, Winter was in her car and about to pull out of the garage. She thought of calling Kody to hear his voice but didn't want to disturb him in case he was already speaking with his client.

A quick have a good day text would have to suffice. Pressing send and placing the phone in the cup holder, she backed out of the garage and started her route to work. Within a few minutes, her phone rang.

"I wanted to see how you slept," Kody said when she answered.

"Not as good as it could have been if someone wasn't so cruel."

"Don't be that way. I'll make it up to you, and you can come as many times as you want. You can even come; however you want, by using my tongue or my dick, your choice."

She laughed. "I forget how blunt you are sometimes, but I like it."

"Good to know. Hey, babe, I have to go; the client just pulled up. I can't wait to see you tomorrow."

"Me either," she said, and they ended the call.

That damn Kody. She was getting wet at that very moment, thinking about the dick or tongue comment he'd just made.

But two could play at that game. She'd follow his little teasing rules when he called again tonight. She had to admit, she liked the idea of him turning her on so descriptively from afar and then coming home to finish the job.

However, once he got home, she would touch and tease him and see how he liked it. Mind made up, she knew just the sexy piece of lingerie that would set the tone.

Arriving at work, she placed her belongings in her office and went to join Lisa with scene setups. When she got there, most of it was almost complete, so she provided assistance with the finishing touches and waiting around to watch the actors do their thing.

This scene was an argument that happened at the dinner table with a powerful mafia family. They were planning how to take vengeance on a dirty cop who had planted evidence against one of their family members.

Most of the food in the scene may have been fake, but it didn't stop the real cravings it was awakening. Winter stared at the pasta, chicken, sauces, cakes and various other foods set before the pretend family and knew she had to have Italian for lunch.

By noon she was starving, and when the director yelled cut for the fifteenth time, she grabbed her purse and went to her car. Vino's was the Italian place she'd settle on to satisfy her pasta needs. It also happened to be close to the area where she met Kody.

Not wanting to waste a second on the attack, she mentally fast-forwarded to seeing Kody for the second time on her doorstep. Thinking about why he showed up also made it register with her that she never did talk to the post office about their apparently unorganized mail carrier.

She shook her head and continued her Kody reverie. Approaching a red light, she saw the scene in her mind again. Kody standing there looking like a sex ad, with his beautiful eyes, captivating smile and always relaxed vibe.

Looking over to her right, she saw the restaurant Quaint. She hadn't been there in a while and needed to make her way back there for some of their yummy pastries.

Through their floor to ceiling windows, she could see couples, families and solo diners sitting opposite of their laptops, enjoying their food.

There was a couple right in front that gave her pause. They were holding hands, and although she couldn't make out the woman, she most certainly could make out the man... Kody.

Chapter 20
Winter

"That bastard," Chloe said. "That's what we're calling him, right? That bastard, cause we are mad at him?"

"Yes, Chloe!"

"But why, I still don't understand? He seems like such a great guy. Maybe he has a good explanation. You should have just went in and confronted him or at the very least called him."

"I don't need level-headedness, Chloe. I need anger, which is why I called you first, not Jessica."

"Noted," she said. "That bastard. So tell me again what happened."

"Well, first, and I didn't remember this until after I got home. He got a call Sunday before we went out, and he took it in another room. He never does that, but I assumed it was no big deal and forgot about it. Then the day I see him at the coffee shop, I had just spoken to him a few hours earlier. He told me he was coming back Wednesday. Why would he suddenly be here that same day? Last, but most certainly not least, who was the woman? I couldn't see her face, and she was wearing a lavender skull hat, and her hair was light brown. Who the hell is she, and why was he holding her hands?"

"Damn, and you sure it was him?"

"Yes. I could see him clearly, and his work truck with the Haven Construction logo plastered across the sides was sitting in the parking lot plain as day."

Chloe exhaled and said, "yeah, sounds kinda guilty, but I wonder what happened?"

Finally sitting on her bed and feeling the tears starting up again, she said. "I don't know, Chloe. All I know is I'm hurting. I couldn't even go back to work yesterday. I told Mr. Sanders and Lisa that I wasn't feeling well, came home and cried most of the night."

"Why didn't you call me?"

"At the moment, I couldn't call anyone. As you see, I couldn't even call him. I was shocked, hurt, confused and the pain of seeing him hours after we had just spoken was just too much for me."

"I get it. Do you think you are going to be able to talk to him soon? You know, confront the situation."
"Of course, I will. I mean, he owes me an explanation. I just can't do it right now. He was due to come back today, and I don't plan on opening the door. I just need a little time to breathe and clear my head."

"Did he at least call?" Chloe asked.

"Not yesterday. Which makes him look that much more guilty because we were supposed to talk last night. He did call today, though, a little while ago. I didn't answer, and he hasn't called again. Probably because he plans on stopping by like nothing ever happened."

The tears began to fall, and she grabbed a tissue. "I'm so stupid, Chloe. I shouldn't even be upset; this is all my fault. Every relationship I have ends in heartbreak; I knew that and went for it anyway."

"You're not stupid. You love him, and he had us all convinced that he loves you too. We all do things in love; sometimes it's just hard to see clearly."

"I just don't know what I'm going to do. I do not want to see him right now. I need a few days, but he will probably press me until I open the door."

"Maybe I can help you out with that," Chloe said

"Are you suggesting I come and stay with you and Derek a few days? No way."

"Actually, I'm suggesting something better. You know I have to go to the Dominican Republic tomorrow for a few days. How about you come with me?"

"I don't know, Chloe."

"Winter, please. It's a great idea. You need to get away and clear your mind to think, and the beach is perfect for that. I will mostly be in meetings, so you'll have the room to yourself, and we can just meet up for dinner in the evenings, and that is only if you feel like it."

"No. I ca…"

"Come on, Winter, I know that sounds like a good plan. Unless you have some things at work that are holding you back?"

She thought it over. A quick beach getaway would be nice, and she didn't have much going on at work for the rest of the week. She could use some of those vacation days that had been piling up.

"Ok. I'm in. What time should I meet you?"

◆◆◆

An hour later, while packing for her trip with Chloe, she heard a knock at the door. She closed her eyes and tried to remain calm. She knew it was Kody, and she wasn't ready.

"Winter?" She heard him call through the door.

She walked to the entryway. "GO AWAY!" she yelled.

"Go away?" she heard him mumble to himself. Even without seeing his face, she could hear the confusion in his tone. Or was it guilt?

"Winter. What's wrong? Are you ok? I tried calling, but you didn't answer."

"I'm fine. But you won't be if you don't leave right now."

"What are you talking about? Can you just open the door so we can talk?"

She let out a twisted but saddened laugh. "No, I can't. Just go away, Kody.

She felt the tears, threatening yet again to overflow. She didn't think she would be able to hold them back as one tear escaped and fell down her face.

"Winter, I—" she heard his phone ring.

Assuming he answered it, she heard the ringing stop and him say, "Hi, Teresa, Do you need me?"

Was he serious! Answering the call, of who she assumed was the mystery girl, right there on her doorstep. The nerve of him! She'd wanted a little more time before she faced him. Falling apart and heartbroken wasn't the preferred way she wanted to do this.

He didn't deserve to see her crying and looking like a sad woman with a broken heart. The plan was to take a little time and collect herself and then see him, but fuck that.

There was no better time than the present because she was angry, and he was about to get a piece of her mind. She yanked the door opened and looked at his face to see… panic.

His expression threw her off guard.

He stepped close to her, gave her a quick kiss on the lips, and then started to back away. "I'm so sorry. I have to go. I will call you as soon as I can."

He ran to his truck, jumped in and drove away. Still frozen by all of the emotions and the lingering feeling of his lips on hers, she stood there stunned, hurt, speechless but more confused than ever.

◆◆◆

It had been three days, and she still hadn't heard from or seen Kody. In this location of the world, seeing him might be a bit challenging, but speaking to him wasn't.

However, she didn't even want to speak to him, which was why she had ignored all his calls and hadn't listened to any of his voicemails. She didn't know if he was still trying to reach her because shortly after arriving at their beautiful resort hotel, she had silenced her phone and put it away.

She needed some distance, and she needed peace. Thanks to her current surrounding on the beach of Punta Cana in the Dominican Republic, she had both.

The scenery and sounds of the beach with its glistening waters had welcomed her with open arms and provided a calming for her rampant thoughts.

She'd done a lot of crying and soul searching there. Mostly, it was about why she always, without fail, chose the wrong men. For that question, she didn't have an answer, but she'd finally reached one for the drama at hand.

She was ready to hear Kody out. Not at that very moment, she still needed that last day of separation to finish her mental preparations, but once she returned.

Since their plane was landing Monday morning, she had decided she would go straight to work from the airport and then speak to Kody that evening once she had gotten home.

If she went home first and saw him, she was 100% positive she would not make it to work for the day.

She may have had more vacation time, but she didn't want to miss more days.

She had meetings planned for the next week, and she needed to prepare for them. All in all, whatever he had to say would be best left said after she had finished her day.

In the past, she didn't run away from problems. Even though she had caught the magician himself, screwing another woman, she still listened to what he had to say. It may have been after quite a few slaps, fuck you's and knee lands to the balls, but she still heard him out. And after he was done, she'd walked away.

But with Kody, the pain was so sharp it could slice right into her, and when she spent too much time thinking about him like she was doing right now, it did just that.

Dragging her mind from thoughts of Kody to focus on the beauty laid out before her, she let the sounds and vivid colors of the ocean overtake her. As the waves shifted and spun in the bluish-green waters, the tension in her shoulders began to dissipate. It was hard to stress while staring at something so mesmerizing.

The clear blue sky and fluffy white clouds offered a slight covering of shade in various spots throughout the beach. Winter had taken up residence in one of those spots while enjoying one of the most delicious mango daiquiris she had ever tasted.

Taking a deep breath to enjoy the breeze, she dug her toes deeper into the silky golden sand. This was truly what she needed. Not just a break to clear her head from the Kody drama, but one from life in general.

With the exception of this week, most of the time, her workload kicked her ass. Rarely did she take some time to get away from it all. In fact, the last time she's been to the beach was right before starting at Movie Box Studios.

She remembers it like it was yesterday. Mr. Sanders had already offered her the job on the spot but then a day later he called her with her actual start date. Congratulating her again and then telling her he looked forward to seeing her Monday, she couldn't stop smiling.

It was a Wednesday, which meant she had five days before she was due to start her job. Excited that she had finally landed the career of her dreams, she conference-called Jessica and Chloe to scream the good news in their ears.

Being the spontaneous soul that she is, Chloe suggested they go out immediately and celebrate in the biggest way possible.

Winter would have just settled for drinks downtown, but Jessica, on board with Chloe's suggestion of something spontaneous, suggested a quick trip to Puerto Rico.

Before Winter could shut the idea down, Chloe pointed out that the flight was only a couple of hours and that they could be on a plane that evening. Promising to have her back by Saturday so she could have all day Sunday to relax and prepare for her big day, Winter agreed.

As soon as Winter set foot off of the plane, she was happy that she'd said yes. The getaway to the captivating, majestic island was certainly well deserved. She had worked long and hard to finally get where she was, and a proper celebration was due.

The memory warmed her and gave her the most genuine smile to have come across her face in days.

A guy walked by shirtless in red and blue swim trunks. He had a nice dark complexion that immediately sent her back to wondering about Kody. What was he doing? How was he? She missed him so bad. His face, his mouth, his hand, his dick… his lying ass!

Nope, she wasn't going to do it. The slicing pain of betrayal was starting its engine yet again as thoughts flooded her mind. Who was Teresa? Why did he have to rush off to her? Was she overreacting? Was he really cheating? Had he just learned he was a father? So much she wanted to understand.

But she had to slow down. She would find out tomorrow after work; she just had to stick with her plan.

Chloe put her money on it being the "surprise you're a daddy" card as an explanation for sneaking around and holding a woman's hands. She didn't think it was cheating because she said it didn't fit with him.

But even with that scenario, Winter wasn't sure.

Didn't he tell her that he only came to Georgia a few times a year? On the other hand, he also said he had sex pretty often. All she had to do was consider Ashley and... Ashley, is that what this was about? Was that who he had met with? But on her doorstep, he'd said Teresa, or maybe she heard him wrong. No, it was definitely Teresa.

The pain was overtaking her again, so she gave up and was back to admiring the ocean and letting the questions of tomorrow wait until tomorrow.

◆◆◆

The beach had done its job... or at least the best job it could, with only being given several days to fix a broken heart. Hugging Chloe goodbye and thanking her for her generosity and friendship, Winter jumped into her car and exited the airport in the direction of Movie Box Studios.

It was most certainly going to be a long day. She had some meetings scheduled, but thankfully they weren't until 1 and 3. Therefore, all she had to do during the morning was prepare, but even that seemed tricky because already she couldn't focus.

She was dreading speaking to him after work and deeply saddened with the possibility of bringing her fantasy life with him to an end.

A small part of her felt no matter what he said, they could get through it. That maybe things weren't as bad as she thought. But that idea faded as all the mistakes of her past relationships assured her that wasn't true.

No longer having the ocean's calming effect as a buffer, she had to deal with the pain and uncertainty head-on. It wasn't going to be fun, be she was going to do it.

Pulling open the door of Movie Box Studios, she began the familiar walk to her office. Catching up to her after only a few steps, Lisa said. "So sorry to bombard you, but one of the clients had to reschedule again, and their only availability was this morning."

Winter's shoulders fell.

"Please tell me your kidding."

"Afraid not. They are waiting in your office right now. Put on a happy face. I think things look promising with them."

Winter rolled her eyes. If we can't trust them to keep their meetings straight, I don't know if we can trust much else.

"True, but what are you going to do," Lisa said, shrugging. "I'm going that way. I'll walk with you."

Arriving in front of her office, she took a few deep breaths and then plastered a smile on her face. Walking in, she turned in the direction of the client seated and stopped dead in her tracks as Kody stood to face her.

Chapter 21
Winter

Pulling Lisa aside, Winter said, "This doesn't look like a client to me."

"True, but it's more important than a client."

"I can't believe you basically conspired against me. You don't know what he's done or if I even wanted to see him."

"You are correct again, but what I do know is a man in love when I see one, and that man is in love."

Winter narrowed her eyes at Lisa.

"Come on, Winter, think about it, you said he demolished your walls to get to your heart. Are you really ready to start building a new one so soon?"

Annoyed at Lisa's words of truth, she said, "I'm going to kill you later."

"Be sure to mention how cute I was on my headstone," Lisa said, walking out of the office and closing the door behind her.

Winter turned to Kody, "what are you doing here?" she said.

"Not letting you avoid me any longer."

"Brave. But can this wait until after work?"

He walked towards her, stopping in front of her. She was surprised that he made no moves to touch her. She desperately wanted him to, but at the same time, she hoped he didn't because she'd fall apart and automatically forgive him.

"It could, but I've waited long enough. If I did something wrong, hiding from me is not the answer," he said.

It was at that moment that she looked at him, really looked at him. He looked so tired and worn down. He hadn't even shaved. The look somehow managed to give him a sexy, rugged appearance that made her want to touch him, but she stayed firm and made no contact.

Deciding to get this over with, she said, "I saw you."

Not following and pushing for her to say more, he said, "saw me…"

"Saw you holding hands with some woman on Tuesday at Quaint. You know, a whole day before you told me you would be coming home?"

"Oh wow," he said, finally getting it.

"Exactly," Winter said, crossing her arms and feeling the anger rising up again.

"You have it all wrong, Winter."

Feeling a slight spark of hope peering through the overshadow of doubt, she said, "how so? Were you not holding a woman's hand at Quaint on Tuesday?"

"Please say you have an evil twin," she thought. "Please."

But his response was much worse and one that she hadn't imagined. "Jackson was in a terrible accident."

The words hit her like a freight train. Covering her mouth, she envisioned the worse, and words seemed to escape her. He wasn't supposed to say that. Maybe that he'd cheated or learned he had a kid, hell, maybe even three kids that he didn't know about. That's what she'd rehearsed a response to. Things that seemed so frivolous compared to this.

He grabbed her hand and pulled her towards him; she moved closer without realizing she'd moved at all. Then, she said, "oh, my goodness, Kody, I'm so sorry. Is Jackson ok?"

Wrapping his arms around her as if he could no longer take the small distance between the two of them, he said, "Yes, he's fine, but for a few days, we weren't so sure he would be."

They moved over to the chairs and took a seat. The exhaustion and stress on his face was very evident and now knowing the source and how she must have added to it, she felt awful. "What happened?" she said.

"Well," Kody began, "about ten minutes after I hung up with you on Tuesday, I got a call from Erica that Jackson was in a horrible accident and he wasn't waking up. I rushed back here and met her at Quaint. You know it's across from the hospital?

A tear rolled down her face as she imagined Jackson hurt and unresponsive. She really liked Jackson, and she knew he and Kody were like brothers. Kody would have taken that hard, and because of her overreacting, she wasn't there to help him. Responding to his question in a sad tone, she said, "yeah, I do. That hospital is the best in the state and I love Quaint's pastries."

Kody laughed. It was nice to see him smile. She imagined he probably hadn't done much of that these last few days.

"So does Jackson, which is why Erica was there. Trying to be optimistic and keep busy, she was getting him a pastry as a surprise for when he woke up."

"Poor Erica. I'm sure she was doing whatever she could just to keep her mind busy. I couldn't imagine."

"Yeah, she was frantic, shaking and throwing up. It's a blur to me now, but I'm sure I probably grabbed her hands at some point to try and calm her."

"And then here I go, losing it over something so innocent. I really am sorry, Kody. I feel horrible. All I knew was I saw you holding some girl's hand. I couldn't make out the girl, but I saw light brown hair and thought the worse."

"Yeah, she colored it."

Winter nodded as she vaguely recalled Erica mentioning wanting to color her hair while they talked about cute celebrity hairstyles at the Super Bowl party.

"It makes sense that you spent time there trying to be there for them both. I really don't know what to say. I wish you would have just told me."

Attempting to lighten the mood, he said, "that would have been like talking to thin air. You wouldn't answer the door or take my calls, remember?"

She looked down at her hands. "Don't remind me," she said. "Well, when you showed up at my door, I would have listened, but you ran off."

"Yeah, that was because I'd gotten a call from the nurse, informing me that Erica had fainted."

The blows just kept coming.

"Please tell me Erica is ok?" Winter said, her voice laced with worry.

"She's fine, great actually. She found out she's eleven weeks pregnant."

"That's wonderful!" Winter said, momentarily forgetting about all the horrors she'd just heard. But all too quickly, they came roaring back—a baby on the way and a husband in the hospital.

"Does Jackson know? Is he awake?"

"Yeah, he woke up on Friday. But by that time, Erica had been checked in because being pregnant and under such stress, she was having blood pressure issues."

"So much has happened in just a few short days. My heart goes out to them, is there anything at all I can do?"

He brushed her cheek with his hand. "No, things are fine. I thank God that they are safe."

"What about you? I should have been there for you. I should have known something was wrong, I should have—"

"Shhh," he pulled her into his arms. "Everything is ok now. They are ok, and we are ok."

She enjoyed the comforts of his embrace. It was a feeling she had missed and longed for repeatedly. She loved him, and it made the hurt of her reaction sting that much more.

Pulling back, she asked, "shouldn't you be seeing about them now instead of hunting down a crazy woman?"

"You may be a crazy woman, but you are my crazy woman."

Giving him a weak smile, she said, "I'm serious, I'm sure they need you. You can go, I'll be alright. I'll even come with you if you'd like."

"No need; they are in great hands. Teresa, who happens to be Jackson's nurse, is also one of their closest friends. She will call me if anything happens."

"That explained who Teresa is," she thought.

She couldn't feel any worse. She'd let her pain and assumptions make her reckless.

All because her past relationships were so shitty.

Sure she couldn't have known he had a logical explanation for everything, but she still felt horrible because he had to handle all of this alone.

He, not even seeming the slightest bit angry, added more weight to her already heavy pile of remorse.

"Why'd he have to be so understanding and calm?" she thought.

"Why are you so easy on me? I know you're a nice guy and all, but I won't lie, I'd be a little annoyed if I were in your shoes."

"Because we are just finding our way, Winter. I knew you'd been hurt when we started this. All you did was put distance between us at what you thought was true evidence of me being unfaithful or lying to you. You were just trying to protect yourself, and I can understand that. It's a slap in the face that you think I could ever hurt you that way, but I get it. However, in the future, can you confront me before running away?"

"After this whole mess, you don't have to tell me twice."

"Where'd you go anyway? I came by on Thursday because I couldn't reach you and Lisa told me you wouldn't be back until Monday because you had a last-minute emergency?"

She sighed. "There wasn't one unless mental issues count. Chloe had a work assignment, and I went with her to spend a few days on the beach and clear my head."

"Gotcha," he said knowingly. "You had to shake off your crazy before returning back to me."

She finally laughed, and before she could say anything more, he kissed her with all the desire, passion and love of a man who needed his woman, and without question, she kissed him with the same.

◆◆◆

It had been several weeks, and Jackson was getting around well. He did need crutches and couldn't stand for long, but even that was a giant leap in the right direction.

"It's my roll," Erica said, tossing the dice onto the board. "Jackson, why are you always cheating? You and Kody buy up all the good stuff before anyone else, and no one has a chance to make much money."

"Umm, it's called Monopoly for a reason," Jackson replied with sarcastic humor.

"You better be glad," Erica said, waving a finger at him.

"Glad that you love me, right?"

"No, glad that I don't want to be a single mom," she said.

They all laughed, and Erica touched her belly. Jackson leaned over to place his hand over hers, and then they gave each other a quick but heartfelt kiss.

"Hey, love birds," Kody said. "I don't mean to put a damper on your moment, but Erica, you rolled a four, which means you are about to owe me some money."

She handed the monopoly money over with fake annoyance. "I'm hungry. You guys hungry?" she asked.

It seemed nowadays Erica was always hungry. But this time, she wasn't alone.

"Yeah," Winter said. "I don't think we ate since breakfast, isn't that right, babe," she asked, looking toward Kody for confirmation.

He was looking down at his phone. "Yeah, I think you're right," he said, only half-listening. "Excuse me for a second; I need to go make a call."

He had been doing that a lot more lately. Leaving to make calls or when the phone rang. She tried not to be concerned with it. It's not like she expected or even wanted him to take all his calls in front of her; she wasn't the jealous type.

It was just strange how his behavior had changed. She could have just asked him, but every time she played the conversation out in her mind, it just sounded so petty.

Jackson decided they should order a pizza, and everyone was on board with that idea. Kody hadn't returned yet, but they all figured he'd be fine with the food of choice, so Winter placed the order.

A few minutes later, Kody returned to the table.

"We ordered pizza," Jackson said. "And I'd like beer with mine, so if you don't mind, can you please grab me one from the fridge."

Jackson was definitely going to milk his situation as much as he could since it meant that he would have his favorite cousin around to wait on him, hand and foot.

Kody stood and said, "I might as well, and while I'm at it, I'll grab one for myself too, you know, since I'm celebrating and all."

Three sets of eyes looked up at him.

"Celebrating?" Winter asked.

"Yeah, I just got off the phone with the managers out in California and Texas. They are completely set to oversee my projects out there. Looks like my days of traveling for work are over."

Jackson let out a loud cheer, while Erica clapped, and Winter looked stunned.

"You mean you no longer plan to travel five months out of the year for work?" Winter asked.

"Nope," he said. "I'm only going to travel as need be, which shouldn't be much at all. I'll go back to California, of course, to put my house on the market and tie up any loose ends, but my new home is here with all of you."

She jumped up and hugged him. She was so happy she could shout. Which is what she did after laying a major kiss on him.

"I'm sorry, babe," he said, still holding her in his arms.

"For what?" she asked.

"All the private phone calls. I wanted to surprise you. I hope it didn't have your mind racing," he said, kissing her on the forehead.

"My mind racing," she said innocently, "oh no, not at all."

◆◆◆

That night, on the ride home, she felt like the luckiest girl in the world. She had everything she could have ever wanted.

Her phone chimed. Looking down, she saw it was a message from Jessica, asking her if they were still on for their spa day tomorrow.

Texting Jessica a reply, she smiled as she thought about how good it would feel to get a massage. It had been a while since her last one, and after her busy schedule at work and helping to take care of Erica and Jackson, she needed it.

But she didn't mind any of the work at all. Her job was still wonderful, and she loved every minute of her time with Jackson and Erica.

The car was slowing, and she looked up from her phone to see Kody pulling over to a deserted park.

"Where are we?" she asked.

He looked at her. "I remember a girl once telling me on this very road that she didn't care if I pulled this truck over and had my way with her. I think it's about time I give that girl what she wants."

With a sly grin, he unlatched his seat belt. She smiled back and did the same.

THE END

Thank you for reading. If you enjoyed this book, we would greatly appreciate a review on Amazon.

If you'd like to be notified when the next book is released you can do so by signing up at
nickigracenovels.com

Keep reading for a preview of the next book in the series!

Inevitable Encounters
Book 2: The Love of my Past, Present

The car wouldn't start. It was the worst time to be having car troubles, but obviously, the universe didn't care because there she was... having them.

She needed to get out of there before she did something she would regret. Her first response was to burn down the house with him and his slut inside of it. Technically speaking, she didn't want to burn down the entire house, just the part where his office was located.

After all, his work was the only thing he really seemed to care about. It was obvious that he didn't care about her. If he did, he wouldn't be upstairs fucking another woman right now. And not just any other woman, Candace.

That skanky, classless, air headed, excuse of a woman, that worked at UpDial Cafe. This girl literally slept with anybody on her quest to become a movie star and now Derek jumps on her list.

Chloe exhaled; she needed to collect herself. She was getting "kill a bitch" angry... again. She had to find a way out of there; obviously, the more time she spent in close proximity to those two assholes, the higher the chances of her new work uniform becoming an orange jumpsuit.

No one would have ever thought, hard-working, sophisticated, beautiful Chloe James could be caught dead in a situation like this.

Sitting in a crappy car, having just discovered that her husband, Derek James, was cheating on her... again. They had basically only been married a year, one year, and this happens.

Her heart was breaking, and her brain was racing.

"Couldn't he even let the ink on the marriage certificate dry before he was off putting his pole, into someone else's hole." Chloe thought.

Her attempt at humor offered no real joy because it hurt too much. She wanted to kill him! She always thought marriage went through issues before the guy gets caught cheating.

Not that having issues were in any way an excuse, but this was straight out of left field. They were in love, and they were newlyweds; how had this happened?

She hit the steering wheel, "DAMMIT DEREK," she yelled.

This all somehow felt like a bad dream that she couldn't wake up from. She felt evidence of its very real existence as another twinge of pain struck from deep inside her. She leaned forward to glance into the rear-view mirror.

A puffy-eyed, mascara streaked face stared back at her. Her light brown eyes, a perfect complement to her creamy brown skin, normally showcased such joy and lighthearted beauty, but at the moment, it only portrayed hurt and sadness.

She looked a mess and felt even worse. She tried to clean herself up, grabbing a piece of tissue from her purse. However, her attempts to improve the condition of her face only made her appear more unkempt.

The waterproof mascara was clinging on for dear life as she kept smearing it further down her face with each swipe of the tissue. She tried wiping slower, then quicker, then slower again, as her patience ran thin.

She felt hopeless and then couldn't stop the fresh wave of tears as they overflowed when the tissue simply broke into tiny, rolled up pieces in her hands. Without looking, she grabbed for more tissues and started wiping frantically again.

Finally stopping to stare at herself, she thought maybe she looked a little better. But it was then, staring at herself in the mirror, that she noticed it...

ABOUT THE AUTHOR

Nicki Grace is an author, wife, mother and philanthropist. She has a Bachelor's Degree in Business Administration and a Master's Degree in Creative Marketing and Entrepreneurship. She enjoys using her skills and background to teach others how to be the best version of themselves.

Made in the USA
Middletown, DE
01 December 2020